Love, LIES & Lemon Pies

STRIPES PUBLISHING
An imprint of Little Tiger Press
1 The Coda Centre, 189 Munster Road,
London SW6 6AW

A paperback original
First published in Great Britain in 2014
Text copyright © Katy Cannon, 2014
Cover copyright © Stripes Publishing Ltd, 2014
Cover photography copyright © Alister Thorpe, 2014

ISBN: 978-1-84715-489-7

A CIP catalogue record for this book is available
from the British Library.

The publisher and author accept no responsibility for accidents,
injuries or damage that may occur as a result of information in this
book. The recipes included here have been tried and tested, and
are correct to the best of our knowledge. Any inadvertent errors or
omissions will be rectified in future editions.

Printed and bound in the UK.

10 9 8 7 6 5 4 3 2 1

Love, LIES & Lemon Pies

KATY CANNON

Stripes

For Gemma, for everything

ABOUT THE RECIPES

The recipes in this book are intended as inspiration. Think of them as a starting point on your baking journey. As Lottie, Mac and the gang learn new techniques, tricks and bakes, I hope you will too. But there's an awful lot more to baking than could fit inside these pages! Experiment with new ingredients and different methods. And I hope you'll research any unfamiliar baking terms or techniques and give them a go.

If you're looking for extra information, there is a world of cookery books and online baking sites at your disposal!

Most of all, I hope your bakes are delicious, and that you share them with your friends and family … and me! I'd love to see photos too.

Katy x

CONTENTS

WHAT YOU NEED TO START

A mixing bowl.

A wooden spoon.

A baking tray or tin.

A recipe.

Some ingredients.

And an oven.

There's lots of baking equipment out there, much of it helpful, some of it not. But when you're just starting out, you don't really need any of it. Baking is something everyone can do. All you really need to begin baking is enthusiasm. And a place to cook…

Home is a funny word.

It means different things to different people. Everyone believes that the way they live, the way their family do things, that's normal. Whatever anyone else does? Just plain weird.

Maybe that means we're all normal, in our own way. And maybe we're all a little bit freakish as well.

Still, say "home" to a group and ask them to define it, and you'll get as many different responses as there are people.

Once they move past the "somewhere to live" thing, and "my family, of course", that's when you start to get the real answers. The ones that matter.

Belonging. Comfort. Relaxation. Space.

For some people, it's a colour. For others, it's the smell of chocolate chip cookies baking. Or the sound of a favourite band blaring out of the radio.

For Grace, it's having somebody else there before her, waiting to welcome her home. For Jasper, a safe,

dark cocoon, where he can be entirely himself –
whoever that is today. For Yasmin, summer sun on
her skin and space to breathe. For Ella, the scent of
her gran's lavender perfume.

Mac claimed home was loud music, the stink of
oil and the feel of metal under his fingertips. He was
lying, but it took us a while to figure that out.

For me? Home is a kitchen. Long clear work
surfaces of stainless steel or gleaming wood. Tiny
bowls of weighed ingredients, laid out ready for me
to mix and fold, stir and create. A shiny silver mixer
and cookie cutters in every shape you can imagine.

In my head, I'm a world-famous baker, with
people queuing for miles just for a taste of one of my
strawberry cupcakes. I'm on the cover of every food
magazine, when I'm not busy starring in my own
cookery programme.

I know, I know. You don't have to tell me. I'm
strange. Especially for a sixteen-year-old girl.

Anyway, the point is, a year ago I didn't know
what home was any more. Now I do, thanks to Bake
Club. And Mac.

GINGER SNAPS

Open packet.

Place on plate.

Serve to unsuspecting students.

The last time I was waiting outside the Head of Year's office was with all the other Junior and Senior Prefects, ready to receive our shiny badges of responsibility. This time, I hadn't got a clue what I was there for, but I had a feeling it wouldn't end with a shiny badge.

Of course, it could be worse. I wasn't the only one waiting outside the office that day, and I guessed the guy sitting across from me was in a lot more trouble than I was.

I'd like to pretend that I didn't know instantly who he was, but Will Macintyre wasn't someone who went unnoticed at our school, even if we hadn't spent four years in the same junior school class. We'd never had classes together since we started secondary school, but he wasn't someone you forgot.

Will Macintyre, Mac to practically the whole school, slumped in the chair opposite me, glaring at his hands. His dark curls fell over his forehead, and he looked as if he were contemplating his future. Which, given what little I knew of Mac, didn't seem very likely.

He looked up, and I wasn't quick enough to look away before he caught me staring. He raised an eyebrow. "Wouldn't expect to see you here. Junior Prefect, and all."

Were those the first words he'd said to me in the past four years? Probably. Guys like Mac didn't talk to girls like me.

He leaned back in his chair when I didn't respond, stretching out his legs in front of him as he eyed me. Just not answering had served me well for the last year. I found eventually people gave up and left me alone.

But not Mac, apparently. Not yet, anyway.

"You're probably here to pick up some award, right? Top marks for everything, or whatever."

I looked away, but didn't answer. Given that my last English essay had only just scraped a B minus, that didn't seem likely.

"Or maybe you have regular chats with our Head of Year," Mac went on. "Filling him in on all the latest gossip, catching up."

He was trying to get a rise from me now. But I'd had a lot more practice at this than him.

Still, maybe it was time to turn the tables.

"What about you?" I asked. "What are you here for today? I mean, as opposed to yesterday. Or every other day. Burn down something new?"

A smile spread across his face.

"So you do know how to talk. I heard people were beginning to think you'd forgotten."

I stared up at the ceiling. I didn't care what people were saying about me. And I had no idea why he of all people was listening to the gossip. "I talk when it's worth my time."

"I'm worth your time?" Mac said, in mock astonishment. "I'm flattered."

I rolled my eyes and looked away. Mac *didn't* matter to me. Maybe that was why I started talking to him. He wasn't part of my world. His friends weren't people I'd hung around with even before the last year. Now I didn't really hang around with anyone. The chances of our lives intersecting again seemed slim. I had two and a half terms left of Year Eleven, and the last half term of that would be study leave and GCSEs. Then I'd be on to sixth form which, at St Mary's at least, seemed like a whole different world.

"You didn't answer my question," I pointed out. "What are you here for?"

"You didn't answer mine, either." Mac folded his hands behind his head and waited.

I looked down at my neatly filed nails. "I heard you smashed up the woodwork room."

Mac's smile widened. "Is that what they're saying? Hell, yeah, I'll take that."

"So it's not true?"

"It's close enough for this school," Mac said.

Which wasn't saying much. St Mary's Secondary School loved a rumour. And I should know. I'd heard enough of them about me and my family over the last year. Of course, none of them hit anywhere near the truth.

"Lottie?" Mr Carroll stuck his head round the door of his office. "Come on in."

Smoothing down my school skirt as I stood, I tried to dismiss Mac from my mind as I entered the tiny room. Mr Carroll was already back behind his desk, stacks of papers and exercise books covering most of the surface between us, and a plate of ginger snap biscuits balanced on top of them.

"Sit down," he said, smiling as if we were friends, as if this were an everyday occurrence. Which it really, really wasn't. "Biscuit?"

Biting my lip, I shook my head, trying to stop my mind from whirling, to think of a reason for the

Head of Year to call me in. My first panicked response had been that something bad had happened. But then I realized if that was the case, he wouldn't have casually asked me to stop by at lunchtime when he saw me in the corridor that morning. I knew exactly what happened when there was a real tragedy. The school secretary, with her big sad eyes, showed up at your classroom, and took you out to where the Head was waiting. I knew because it had happened to me a year ago.

"I'm sure you've got an idea why I asked you to come in today," Mr Carroll said, selecting a ginger snap from the plate.

I stayed quiet. I didn't think *I haven't a clue* was the answer he was looking for.

Unfazed by my lack of response, Mr Carroll sat back in his chair and studied me, exactly as Mac had done. The comparison made me want to laugh, but that probably wasn't the reaction Mr Carroll wanted, either.

"I've had a number of your teachers speak to me over the last few months," he said after a moment. "All concerned about you."

"I'm fine," I said. My default answer in these situations.

Mr Carroll flipped open a file. "You've dropped

out of all your after-school activities, even the band. You've given up your Junior Prefect duties, which makes your chances of being appointed a Senior Prefect in sixth form slim. You've stopped volunteering at school fundraisers, stopped taking part in events and assemblies."

"That's because my GCSEs are coming up," I said. "My mum and I thought I should focus on my school work." It was almost the truth. Mum probably hadn't noticed I'd dropped anything. But the focus part was true. I needed good grades if I wanted to get away from home and do ... something.

"Which would be admirable, except your grades are erratic too." Mr Carroll's eyebrows furrowed slightly as he read through my file, chewing on his biscuit. "Even in subjects you've always loved and excelled at. Your teachers say you seem to have lost enthusiasm for everything."

"It's been a hard year," I said, and stared straight at him, watching as he fumbled to turn the page. "I'm sure you can appreciate why I might be feeling a little less enthusiastic than normal."

"Of course," he said. "You know how very sorry we are for your loss. And, as a community, the school has tried to be as supportive as it can since your father ... passed. But..."

There was a "but"? How could there be a "but"? Mine had to be the best possible reason for not wanting to get stuck into school shows and harvest fairs. How could they possibly expect those things to matter to me when Dad was dead?

"But we're worried about you," Mr Carroll finished, and I felt some of my annoyance fade.

"I'm fine," I repeated, a bit more firmly this time, and reached for a ginger snap, as if that would prove it.

"Are you?" Leaning forward to rest his elbows on the desk, Mr Carroll gave me a solemn, concerned look. "Lottie, you've been through more than any teenager should have to this past year. It's understandable that you might look at school, and life, and people differently. But turning inward isn't the answer. When times are hard, you need people around you, you need support and friendship and help."

Obviously Mr Carroll had no idea exactly how unhelpful my friends had been, letting me push them away because they couldn't cope with me and my grief. But I didn't need them. Besides, friends weren't the problem. The problem was that I spent so long trying to make every assignment perfect, re-copying my notes until they were flawless, that I ran out of time to do everything. Which usually left me with one or two model assignments, and four or five rushed ones.

"I've spoken with your form tutor, and she confirms that you've been withdrawn for months now. Maybe even depressed. She said you'd lost weight…"

"I have not!" I took a defiant bite of my biscuit.

"Well, regardless. I spoke to the school guidance counsellor, and she agreed that you could benefit from some sessions with her."

I felt the first pangs of panic in my chest, but when I started to object, Mr Carroll simply held up his hand and spoke over me. "I know you saw a counsellor last year, but I think talking to someone again could help, now some time has passed."

"I don't need a counsellor," I said. "I'm fine."

Mr Carroll sighed. "No, Lottie, you're not."

"So this is compulsory?"

"Until we can see that you're interacting more, being part of the school again, putting effort into your classes… Yes, I'm afraid it is."

I searched for an argument, something I could use to stop this, but came up blank. Apparently just telling people I was fine wasn't proof enough any more.

"Mrs Tyler, the counsellor, also suggested that it

might be worthwhile for her to talk to your mum. Either here at the school or, if it's more comfortable, maybe at your house?"

"No!"

That absolutely could not happen. Ever.

I don't know if the horror I felt came across in my voice, but Mr Carroll obviously saw a weakness and latched on to it.

"Mrs Tyler has very close ties to social services," he went on, watching me carefully. "Even if you don't think you need to talk to someone, perhaps your mum does. After all, she lost someone as well."

And she gained so much more. The joke bubbled up and I swallowed down my urge to laugh hysterically. This was serious. This was dangerous.

I needed a way out. A way to convince them I was fine.

Chewing on the inside of my cheek, I called on my Drama Club training – another abandoned hobby – to act unhappy but resigned. Mr Carroll needed to believe I was opening up to him, even if really I wasn't.

"Mr Carroll, look. I know I've been a bit … distracted lately. And I know that this year is important, and I need to get my grades back up. But it's been really hard reconnecting with my friends, after everything." I paused for maximum effect before saying, "I know I have to … move on, eventually. I just don't think I can go back to being exactly who I was before."

I glanced up to see if he was buying it and, behind his softening features, I spotted a flyer pinned to his noticeboard. That flyer changed the whole year for me. It had a picture of a cupcake, decorated with jolly pink sprinkles, and the words *Bake Club* in a curly font underneath. Suddenly I remembered Miss Anderson talking about the new club she was starting, for Year Tens and Elevens who wanted to learn to bake, even if they weren't taking food tech GCSE.

"I want to start something new," I said, looking at him with conviction. "Which is why I thought I'd join the new Bake Club after half-term."

"The Bake Club?" Disbelief coloured Mr Carroll's voice.

"Absolutely," I said, beginning to warm to the idea. "My dad and I always used to bake together. It's something I've really missed this year." A good dose of truth to help convince him. I had missed baking. And when Miss Anderson had announced the new club I'd thought, just for a moment, about joining. Before the thought of actually having to deal with other people put me off. Still, if I had to convince the school that I was a normal girl with interests and hobbies, Bake Club could work. It was new, so I wouldn't be walking into a group that already had its own cliques and rules. And it was being run by Miss Anderson, the new food technology teacher who'd just moved from America at the start of the year, who I liked.

And, on top of everything else, it would give me an excuse to stay away from home for an hour or two longer, at least one day a week. An advantage not to be ignored.

"It might even help me with my food tech GCSE," I added.

"Well, that's … good, then." Mr Carroll frowned again. "But I still want you to keep these appointments with Mrs Tyler." He handed me a slip of paper with some times printed on it and a room number.

I took the paper with reluctance. In the space of ten minutes, I'd become the guidance counsellor's pet project, as well as a wannabe baker. But as long as it kept her – and social services – out of my house, I wasn't going to complain.

Dismissed at last, I walked out of the office, Mr Carroll following close behind. I heard him sigh as he opened the door to stare out at Mac.

"Mr Macintyre," he said wearily. "You'd better come in."

I raised my eyebrows at Mac, who casually got to his feet as if he were doing Mr Carroll a favour by being there at all. "Have fun," I said.

He rolled his eyes. "Yeah, sure. Maybe they'll even kick me out this time."

Maybe they would. Maybe his luck had run out and whatever he'd done would be enough to get him expelled.

But it wasn't.

And it turned out I'd just given Mr Carroll a much better idea for Mac's punishment.

CHOCOLATE CHIP COOKIES

1. Heat the oven to 180°C/fan 160°C/gas 4.
2. Cream together 125g of softened unsalted butter and 200g of light muscovado sugar in a bowl using a mixer, or wooden spoon.
3. Mix in 1 tsp of vanilla extract and a lightly beaten egg.
4. Sift in 200g of plain flour, ½ tsp of baking powder and a pinch of salt.
5. Stir until just combined, then fold through 200g of chocolate chips.
6. Place spoonfuls of cookie mixture on to a greased and lined baking tray, making sure to leave room for spreading.
7. Bake for 15 to 20 minutes, until they turn a pale golden colour.

I wasn't really prepared for how much courage it would take to walk into the food tech classroom that first week. I'd grown too used to staying out of things, to being alone. But I've always been stubborn; I'd said I would join Bake Club and so I had to go. Of course, that didn't stop my heart banging around my ribcage as I neared the classroom. Head high, shoulders straight, just like Dad had always taught me, I pushed open the door and walked in.

For a brief moment, the room fell silent as the other students looked up and saw me. Miss Anderson glanced at me and smiled, but then turned her attention back to the paper on her desk. And then, of course, the whispers started. The same *hiss hiss* noise I'd heard all year. People didn't know what to say to my face, so they whispered it behind my back. As if I couldn't guess exactly what they were saying anyway.

I ignored it, just like I'd been doing for the last twelve months, not stopping to look around until

I reached the empty workstation at the back of the room. I was taking part, just like I'd promised Mr Carroll. I didn't have to like it.

From my position, I could see everyone – or at least the backs of their heads. The room was split into back to back workstations on either side, with sinks between them, set in counters that ran against the classroom wall. There were twelve in total.

Leaning against the workstation in front of me was Yasmin, an Indian girl I'd been partnered with in geography once in Year Eight, who had spent the whole time talking about her older brothers, one in the army, the other applying to study at Oxford. Across from her was Jasper, known throughout the school as "that weird Goth kid" since he'd shown up on the first day of this term with his blond hair dyed jet black. And on the other side of the room, at the workstation nearest Miss Anderson's desk, was Grace. The pretty one. The popular one. The queen of Drama Club, who'd barely acknowledged my existence even *before* I chose to become a social outcast. I should have known she'd want to rule this group too.

Miss Anderson clapped her hands together and the murmurings fell silent. "I'm so delighted to see you all here today! When I said I wanted to start a baking club, well … not everyone thought it would get off the ground. So thank you for proving me right." She beamed as she glanced round the classroom and I looked away before she caught my eye. "My inspiration for the club, actually, was this." When I looked back, Miss Anderson was holding up a brightly coloured poster, with a garishly decorated cake on the front, and the words *National Schools' Bake-Off* written in a swirly font that looked a bit like icing. "It's a big new contest and parts of it might be featured on television!"

The faces of the kids around me didn't echo her enthusiasm. In fact, everyone looked faintly horrified at the prospect. Myself included.

Judging the mood of the crowd, Miss Anderson put the poster down. "Anyway. We'll see how we get on. But I'll send off for the information pack, just in case." She clapped again. "Right, then. Take your seats and we'll get started. Since it's our first week, I thought we'd go with a classic. As you can see, I've got three stations set up with all the necessary ingredients. Next week, I'll need you to bring your own, but today I've supplied them for you."

Three stations and four students meant somebody had to share. Thank God I'd grabbed the lonely one at the back. Jasper jumped up from his stool, obviously realizing at last that the workstation he'd sat down at didn't have the same recipe card and ingredients that the others did. He glanced around him and I held my breath until he grinned at Yasmin, joining her on the other side of their stations. I was still alone.

At least, until the door flew open again and Will Macintyre barrelled in, all untucked shirt and messy dark hair.

"Ah, Will. You made it." Miss Anderson actually seemed pleased to see him, unlike any other teacher at St Mary's. "We're just about to start. Why don't you team up with Lottie, at the back?"

And, just like that, my quiet baking time was over.

As Miss Anderson started talking us through some baking basics I already knew, I took the opportunity to watch the boy who'd claimed a fifty per cent share in my chocolate chip cookies. He looked in an even worse mood than he had earlier in the week outside Mr Carroll's office.

"And now, it's over to you," Miss Anderson said, with a little more excitement than I felt was strictly necessary. "Just follow the recipe and you'll be fine."

At our station, Mac turned to me and scowled. "You're just everywhere this week, aren't you?"

"Apparently so." I gave him a too-bright smile.

"Aren't you lucky?"

"I was going to go with cursed," Mac said, but his scowl lightened up a bit, so I figured he was probably joking.

"You ever made cookies before?"

Mac shrugged. "Never made much of anything before."

I paused with my fingers about to reset the scales and looked up at him. "Sooo ... what are you doing here, then? Experienced a sudden urge to learn about pastry, or something?"

His laugh was sharp, with no humour in it. "Yeah, right," he said, sarcasm dripping from his words. "You don't think I'd be doing this by choice, do you? Not all of us want to spend our free time at school."

I busied myself with the flour again. I wasn't there by choice, whatever he thought. But I didn't want Mac asking questions about why I had to attend. Better for him to think I just loved baking. Which, actually, was sort of the truth. Now I was back in the kitchen, I was beginning to remember all the things Dad and I had loved about baking together. Even before cupcakes became cool and people started competing on national TV to make the best Battenberg, my dad was teaching me how to bake, the same way his mum taught him.

So, while other dads taught their kids to throw a ball or mow the lawn or whatever, mine taught me to dust berries in flour before folding them into the muffin mix, and how to pipe perfect icing.

Maybe a club wasn't my sort of thing any more. But there was a definite appeal in rediscovering the fun of being up to your elbows in icing sugar. Since Dad died there hadn't been many opportunities for cake making. Or fun.

"So, why are you really here?" I asked Mac, wondering if he'd confirm my suspicions about Mr Carroll making him come. While I waited for an answer, I measured the chocolate chips into a bowl. With every ingredient neatly weighed and arranged in order of use in front of me, I was almost ready to start baking.

Mac ignored my question entirely. Boosting himself up to sit on the counter, he said, "You know no one else is doing this, right?"

"Doing what?" I straightened the bowls, and set about reading through the recipe again. Whatever Mac's reasons for being there that afternoon, they clearly didn't involve helping me make cookies. He hadn't even put on an apron.

He waved his hand over the counter. "Whatever you're doing with the fiddly little bowls."

"It's important to weigh out your ingredients

before you start," I said. But, looking around, it was clear that no one else had bothered. Not even Miss Anderson, working with Grace at the front. Bags of flour and sugar and chocolate chips lay strewn across Yasmin and Jasper's counter, and they were arguing over the mixing bowl. I looked at my neat bowls and alphabetized bags of ingredients. Yeah, OK, so I was a freak. But a freak with *logic*.

"If you have everything ready in advance, there's less chance of surprises while you're baking."

"Surprises can be good." A smile spread across Mac's face. The sort of hinting, taunting smile I hate.

I reached for the butter. "Not in my experience."

"Then clearly you don't have much experience."

My cheeks burned. Why did I have to blush so easily. I turned to tip the butter into the mixing bowl, hoping Mac wouldn't notice my red face, but from the way his grin widened even further, he did.

"So, what do we do?" Mac asked, peering over my shoulder at the recipe. "*Cream butter and sugar? What the hell does that mean? Sounds dirty...*"

I tried to keep a straight face, and failed. "Why am I not surprised that's the first thing you think of?"

He smirked back at me. "Admit it. You were thinking it too."

I didn't answer that one. "All it means is that we

have to beat them together until they're creamy." I glanced around the classroom. There were only two stand mixers in the class and since the others hadn't bothered getting their ingredients in order, they were already both in use. At one, Miss Anderson and Grace had their heads bent over the mixing bowl, talking quietly. At the other, Jasper was gleefully tipping in chocolate chips, while Yasmin tried to brush flour off her school uniform.

"We'll have to wait for a turn with one of the stand mixers. Unless there's a hand one in here somewhere..." I started opening cupboards under the counter, but Mac leaned across me, and I could feel the warmth of his body over mine.

"Says here we can use a wooden spoon," he said, brandishing one. "Hand over the bowl."

I clutched the mixing bowl against my apron. "We *can*, but it's hard work and it takes forever. Be quicker to wait for a mixer." Which wasn't quite the same as saying, *I'm a lazy weakling*, but probably came close.

Mac tapped the counter with his spoon. "Give it here."

Reluctantly, I passed the bowl to him, with its perfectly measured and weighed, cubed room-temperature butter inside, ready for beating.

I managed almost a minute of watching him bash

at the butter with the spoon before I grabbed it back. "Not like that. Like this." Demonstrating, I pressed through the butter with my spoon, beating it smooth until my arm burned with the ache.

"I got it." Mac grabbed the bowl and copied my movements perfectly, only stronger and faster.

Miss Anderson wandered past, doing the rounds, checking in to see how we were doing. "That's looking great, Will," she said.

He glared at her. "It's Mac. Everyone knows that."

Miss Anderson's permanent happy face slipped. "Well, you know, I'm new here. I'll remember for future," she said, and she moved on towards Jasper and Yasmin.

"She's nice, you know," I said.

"She's a teacher." Mac shoved the bowl towards me. "What's next?"

"OK, so now we add in the sugar." Selecting the next bowl from my line-up, I poured in the sugar and motioned for Mac to start beating again, trying not to feel too guilty about wimping out. After all, we were partners today. He was *supposed* to be helping, and I'd already done all the prep work.

"So why are *you* here?" Mac asked, turning the question he hadn't answered back on me. Sneaky. "I mean, you obviously already know how to do this

34

stuff. Why not just bake at home?"

I turned to straighten the bottle of vanilla extract so the label faced the front. "Thought I might learn some new techniques, maybe. And baking at home can be kind of lonely."

I hadn't meant to add that last part. I mean, it was true – since Dad died, baking alone didn't hold so much appeal. But that wasn't why I didn't do it. And besides, being alone hadn't been a problem until Mr Carroll made it one.

Mac didn't get the chance to press any further, because Jasper popped up beside our station, leaning over the worktop to get a look in our bowl. "Is that easier than using the mixers?"

"No," Mac and I both answered.

"Damn. I figured something had to be." Jasper leaned forward even further, and I rescued the bag of sugar from his path before it went flying.

"What problems are you having with the mixer?" I asked.

Jasper gestured to his shirt. "Everything just keeps flying out!"

Handing him a damp cloth, I said, "Let me guess. You dumped all the flour in at once?"

"The recipe said 'add flour'," Jasper said defensively, as he dabbed at his shirt. "So I added the flour."

"It works better if you add it a bit at a time. Or even fold in the flour by hand." It felt natural discussing baking techniques, in a way I hadn't expected. Apparently talking to people was one of those skills you didn't forget. Or maybe Mac and Jasper were just easier to talk to than my old friends.

Jasper gave me a curious look. "How do you know this stuff?"

"She's a master baker," Mac told him. "Why do you think I paired up with her?"

"Because Miss Anderson told you to," Jasper said, before flashing me a grin and heading back to Yasmin.

I shook my head. Despite his Goth appearance, he acted like an eager puppy. I heard him yelling, "Lottie says we were doing it wrong," as he went.

Great. Now Yasmin would think I was a know-it-all. Normally I wouldn't care, but I was pretty sure Mr Carroll – or the guidance counsellor – would want a report on all the new friends I'd made at Bake Club. Which probably meant I should make some.

Mac ignored Jasper's yelling, choosing instead to shove his mixing bowl under my nose. "This done yet?"

Amazingly, it was. Pale and creamy and perfect. It would have taken me three times as long to do it by hand. "You must have good muscles," I said, then winced. "I mean…"

But this time, Mac either didn't notice my blush or ignored it. "It's working at my dad's garage that does it."

I'd never thought much about what Mac did in his spare time. If I had, I'd have guessed troublemaking and possibly criminal damage as his favourite hobbies, given his record. The idea of him actually working took me a little by surprise.

"I guess cars are more your sort of thing than cakes." I poured in the vanilla extract and the beaten egg, then waved a hand to tell him to mix again. It was like having my very own, gorgeous, human KitchenAid.

"Cars, I understand." Mac nodded towards the recipe card. "This stuff makes no sense to me."

"That's only because you haven't learned. Baking techniques can't be any harder than fixing a car." He didn't look convinced, so I went on. "I mean, with a car, once you know what's wrong, what's supposed to be where, and what does what, you can make it work, right?"

"If it's fixable." Mac held out the bowl again and I took it from him, setting it on the counter and placing the sieve on top.

"Well, baking's the same. I know if I sieve the flour in, it'll give the mixture more air, and make my cookies lighter. Once you know what to do and why, it all comes down to practice." I might not have practised much in the past year, but Dad's lessons were ingrained. As soon as I'd stood in that classroom, everything had started to come back to me. "When you've got the basics down, it's all just following instructions."

"I never was very good at that." Mac gave me a lopsided grin. "There are usually so many more fun things to do."

I really wasn't going to think about what a guy like Mac did for fun.

"Well, follow these instructions and you get cookies."

"There is that." Mac held out the bowl. "Do I get to sample the chocolate chips?"

"I have exactly the right quantity of chips for this recipe," I told him sternly. "Do not mess with the ingredients."

He pulled a sad face, but tipped in all the chocolate chips anyway.

"If we're ready," Miss Anderson called across the class, "the oven is at temperature. Bring me your baking trays, and I'll pop them in for you."

"We're not ready, are we?" Mac asked, looking into the bowl with confusion.

I pulled out my greased and lined baking tray. "Nearly. We just need to spoon the mixture on to here."

"Even I can do that." Mac grabbed the wooden spoon and dolloped a huge blob of cooking dough on to the tray, scraping it off the spoon with his fingers.

"Not like that!" There was, I'll admit, a hint of a shriek in my voice. But in my defence, he was *doing it all wrong*.

"Then how?" Mac asked, exasperated.

"Like this." Pulling two teaspoons from the drawer, I showed him how to fill the tray with evenly sized balls of dough, each perfectly spaced to allow for spreading while they cooked.

"How do you get them all the same size?"

"Practice." Eyeing the tray, I spotted one cookie dollop with more chocolate chips and fished one out to press it into a cookie with fewer.

"Perfectionism," Mac countered.

I ignored him. "Want to take these over to Miss Anderson?" I asked. "After all, you did all the hard work."

Mac pushed the tray towards me. "Only because you told me what to do. You take them."

The chocolate chip cookies only took twenty minutes to bake, which was supposed to give us time to clear up. Instead, when I got back from talking to Miss Anderson about the best way to rotate the trays to ensure even baking, I found the rest of the group standing around my neat and tidy workstation.

"We're doing *A Midsummer Night's Dream* in Drama Club," Grace said, as I tried to get past them to the sink to start washing up. "You should think about auditioning, Mac."

Mac snorted, but moved out of my way at least. "I think one after-school club is enough for me, don't you?"

"How did you get roped into this, anyway?" Jasper asked, obviously as curious as me about Mac's sudden interest in baking.

I tried not to look guilty. But Mac just shrugged. "Wrong place at the wrong time," he said, which was possibly more true than he knew.

"Well, I'm partnering with Lottie next week." Jasper grinned at me. "She's the one who really knows what she's doing." Apparently Mac's "master baker" comment meant I'd be spending a lot of time showing other people what to do.

"And right now," Miss Anderson called, "she's doing the washing up, like I asked you all to."

There were a few grumbles as people wandered back to their incredibly messy workstations, but Mac just grabbed a tea towel and started drying the bowls I'd already washed. And by the time we were done, the timer was going off to tell us the cookies were ready.

"We really should let them cool…" Miss Anderson started. Then she smiled. "But they do taste best warm." Sliding them off the trays on to plates, she let us dive in.

I held back a moment, wanting to choose the right cookie, but before I could even get close enough to figure out which one looked best, Mac handed me one. It was too big, crispy at the edges and soft in the middle, with the chocolate chips unevenly spread through it. It could only be the result of Mac's overenthusiastic dolloping of dough on to the tray.

"My first home-made cookie," he said. "Seemed only fair that you get to eat it."

"I'm so, so honoured," I said.

And actually, I was.

CLASSIC VICTORIA SANDWICH

1. Heat the oven to 180°C/fan 160°C/gas 4.
2. Cream together 200g of unsalted butter and 200g of caster sugar.
3. In another bowl, lightly beat 4 eggs with ½ tsp of vanilla extract.
4. Slowly add the egg mixture to the butter and sugar, beating after each addition.
5. Sift in 200g of self-raising flour and 1 tsp of baking powder, then fold through the mixture.
6. Spoon the mixture equally into two 20cm sandwich tins and spread to the edges.
7. Bake for 20 to 25 minutes, until the cakes are golden brown and springy on top.
8. When cool, sandwich together with strawberry jam and, if you like, buttercream.
9. Dust with icing sugar to finish.

The following Thursday, I was stupidly excited about Bake Club. Which just shows you the depths of ridiculousness I'd sunk to in the intervening seven days.

I knew that one baking session with a guy didn't mean anything. We weren't friends – I'd barely even seen Mac since, apart from once, from a distance, standing outside Mr Carroll's office again. But there was, in my mind, the *possibility* of friendship. After spending a year ignoring everyone, letting my old friends drift away until they formed new groups without me, I couldn't deny that it felt good to talk to someone. Even if it was just about chocolate chips.

I didn't let myself think about anything more than a baking-based friendship. Not just because a guy like Mac wouldn't be interested in a nonentity like me. But because I really wasn't interested in a relationship with him. I mean, yeah, he was gorgeous. And he'd been nicer than I'd expected. But the last thing I needed was to get involved with someone like Mac.

To remind myself of this, I ran through what I knew about Will Macintyre, school rebel.

One. The arson. Mac once set fire to some guy's car. That wasn't even just a rumour. A kid with a relative in the local police had confirmed it. And when asked about it, Mac had apparently glared and said, "What's it to you if I did?" – which was as good as a confession. He'd been thirteen at the time. Maybe we shouldn't be letting him near the school ovens.

Two. Um…

…He looked really good while mixing cookie dough?

I paused for a moment, leaning against a display board filled with flyers. Was that really all I knew about Mac? I was as bad as all those kids who only knew me as "that girl whose dad died".

Maybe that was just how secondary school worked. There were too many kids to get to know everyone, and we were all too tied up with our own issues to care about anyone else's. So we learned to put people in boxes based on the one thing we knew about them, whether that was that they loved computer games, or did drama, or had once set fire to a car.

If I wanted to convince Mr Carroll I belonged in this school again, I had to start paying more attention to the people around me. And *before* my first meeting with the guidance counsellor.

I'd forgotten Jasper's plan to partner with me that week. When I finally made it into the food tech classroom, still buzzing a little with anticipation, there was a change from the week before. We'd gained a person.

At the workstation I'd used last week, Mac sat on the counter talking to a pale, petite, blond girl I vaguely recognized from the year below us. Miss Anderson had declared that Bake Club was for Years Ten and Eleven only – the younger classes had a Cupcake Club – but nobody in Year Ten had seemed very interested.

I glanced around the rest of the room. Yasmin and Grace had teamed up at another station and Jasper was motioning me over to his, calling, "Lottie! Over here!"

Miss Anderson looked up. "Lottie, great! You're here. Looks like you're working with Jasper this week."

I grabbed an apron from the pegs, slipped it over my head and tied it round my waist. So I was starting my new get-to-know-people campaign with Jasper.

Taking in the oversized black hoodie slung over his school uniform, and the black eyeliner round his puppy dog eyes, I told myself this was going to be fun.

Miss Anderson trailed after me to Jasper's workstation. "Um, Lottie…"

I paused and turned to her, my standard polite pupil face in place. "Yes?"

"Mr Carroll asked me to pass on a message for you. Mrs Tyler's off this week, so she won't be able to see you until next week."

Mrs Tyler. The school counsellor. I glanced back over my shoulder, just in time to see Jasper looking away. Trying to pretend he hadn't been listening.

"Oh, right. Fine. Thanks." I kept my head down, and pretended I didn't see Miss Anderson watching me for a long moment.

Finally, she walked back to the front of the classroom and clapped her hands together. "I'm so glad to see you all back here this week," she said. "And we've even gained a new member! Hello, Ella." She gave a little wave, and the girl, Ella, smiled nervously back. "It's lovely to have someone here from Year Ten. Maybe you can convince some of your friends to join too!"

Miss Anderson asked us all to get out the laminated

recipe cards we'd been given last week. "This week we're going to be making a classic Victoria sandwich. So I hope you've all brought your ingredients. I've got enough tins for everyone, but I'm afraid you're sharing mixers again until I convince the school committee to let us buy some new ones."

That wouldn't be a problem for Ella, anyway. Not with Mac the human mixer as her partner.

I bit the inside of my cheek. Baking a batch of chocolate chip cookies together didn't make Mac mine. And I was never going to fit in well enough to get Mr Carroll off my back if I started being bitter and jealous.

"You know how to do this, right?" Jasper asked me, as he peered at the printed text like it was in a foreign language. "Because honestly, I haven't a clue."

"I do." Reading through the recipe once to be sure, I started putting my ingredients in order, as I reconsidered my plan for the afternoon. OK, maybe I wasn't going to have the chance to find out all Mac's secrets, but Jasper would be a good trial run. I could find out why he wanted to join Bake Club, when he obviously hadn't done much baking before, and wasn't taking food tech. And it wasn't like I couldn't make a Victoria sandwich with my eyes closed anyway.

"So … you're seeing Mrs Tyler?" Jasper asked, apparently unable to contain his curiosity.

I bent down to grab the sandwich tins, so I didn't have to look Jasper in the eye as I lied to him. "Compulsory follow-up session. It's a year since … my dad."

Jasper bought it. "Oh. Yeah, right. Sorry about that."

The silence was awkward for a moment, until Jasper lurched in to fill it again. "Where did you learn cake making?"

"From my dad actually. His mum taught him, he taught me. Kind of a family tradition." As I cubed the butter, I decided to turn the tables. "Is that why you're here? To learn how to bake?" You'd have thought it would be obvious, but since my sample group so far was me and Mac, I knew it wasn't always the case.

Jasper pulled a face. "Kind of, I suppose."

"And you sound so enthusiastic about the idea!" I teased. "I don't get it. Why would anyone join a baking club if they didn't want to bake? Also, sugar, please."

Jasper passed me the bag. "Lots of reasons. Yasmin told me she's here because it's quieter than at her house. Grace … who knows. I don't even pretend to understand that girl."

I glanced over at Yasmin and Grace's station. As far as I could tell, Yasmin was doing most of the work, while Grace just looked bored. When she wasn't staring at Mac. I followed her gaze and Jasper obviously did the same.

"As for Mac … I heard that he got kicked out of the design technology class just before half-term, and has to take food technology to make up his timetable. Mr Carroll said he'd only let him switch if he joined Bake Club."

OK, it was definitely my fault Mr Carroll had the idea to stick Mac here. *Oops.*

Ingredients all weighed and prepared, I tipped the butter into the stand mixer and turned it on, its reassuring whirring making me feel like all was right in the world.

Not that I wouldn't have swapped it in a heartbeat for watching Mac mix the cake.

"So what about you?" I asked, over the noise.

"Me?" Jasper spread his arms wide. "I'm rebelling."

"Through baking."

He grinned at me. "It could happen."

I tried to put myself in Jasper's place, and imagine

what would make a weird skinny Goth kid want to learn to make cakes.

"I think it's something else," I said, after a moment. "Come on, you can tell me. What is it? Baking a cake to impress some girl? Trying to make it up to your mum for never cleaning your room? What?"

Turning away, he fiddled with the recipe card in his hand. "I told you. I'm rebelling. Sort of."

"I don't understand."

Jasper dropped the card to the counter. "I'm here because I'm avoiding my parents and the idea of me baking will give them something else to obsess about and analyse."

Now I was lost. "Your parents? They like to analyse … stuff?"

"Me," Jasper said glumly. "They like to analyse me."

"OK…" I said, still not understanding a word he was saying. Did this boy ever make any sense? While I waited for an explanation, I checked the mixer. The butter had reached the perfect pale creaminess, so I poured in the sugar.

"They're psychologists," Jasper explained, as the mixer got to work. "They like to think they understand everything about the human psyche. They've been waiting for me to hit the teenage years ever since I was born. I think they see it as a challenge."

"That's a bit weird." Not that I could talk. But still...

Jasper gave me a sad smile. "Yes. Yes, it is."

So maybe that explained the Goth look too. Jasper certainly wasn't your typical angry kid listening to death metal. Too ... happy, most of the time. But if it was just to give his parents something to analyse, it made a strange kind of sense. I still wasn't sure where the baking fitted in, but my mission to get to know my fellow bakers was off to a good start. I was about to ask how cake making helped his parents' analysis, when Mac dropped his wooden spoon on the counter with a clatter, and strode across to our workstation.

"Jasper, mate, you've got a new partner," he said. "Come on."

For a brief moment, I actually thought that Mac was sending Jasper to partner Ella, so he could share with me. And from the way Jasper's eyes lit up as he looked over at Ella, so did he.

But then Mac motioned to Ella, and she shyly slipped from behind their counter to stand just behind him.

"Lottie, Ella needs someone who can actually do this. So she's going to pair with you, OK?"

51

I blinked. "What about Jasper?"

Mac sighed as he looked across at Jasper. "Looks like we'll have to muddle through it together. See if anything you taught me last week stuck." He winked at me, motioned for Jasper to follow, and headed back off to the other station.

Will Macintyre had winked at me. I took a moment to process it, before turning to Ella, who stood nervously in front of me. I glanced up at Miss Anderson, who appeared to be too engrossed in a conversation about the merits of KitchenAid over Kenwood with Grace to have noticed the switch.

"Looks like it's you and me, then," I said. "I'm Lottie, as Mac probably told you before he stole my partner."

Ella winced. "Sorry about that. I just... I think he's trying to help me."

Which was funny, because that's what I thought too. Something new to add to the short list of things I knew about Mac. Sometimes, he tried to help people. Who knew?

"You see, the thing is..." Ella trailed off and looked up at me, smile just a little too tight. "It's silly really. My gran promised to make a cake for this week's Mothers' Union meeting at church and she makes the best cakes ever. But she's come down with a bug – you know, sore throat, cold, that sort of thing – and she doesn't feel up to baking. So I said I'd do it for her. Only..."

"You don't know how."

She nodded. It made sense, sort of. But her eyes looked a little too desperate, and her hands were clenched together too tightly.

She was lying to me. I had absolutely no idea why, but she obviously really needed this cake. "So you need me to make you a cake to take to the meeting. Couldn't you just buy one?"

Ella gave me a look. "They'd know. They always know. Gran says that one Christmas someone tried to pass off M&S mince pies as their own. They got kicked out."

"Well, it's a good job I know how to make a perfect Victoria sandwich, then. Do you want to pass me the bowl with the eggs?"

Ella stared at the ingredients for a long moment, then handed me the bowl. "Thanks for helping me," she said, as I spooned the first tablespoon of egg mixture in. "Does that look right? Is it curdling?" She leaned closer as I continued adding the egg.

"It's fine." And it was, of course. It was my cake.

"Only, my gran is always worried about mixtures curdling." Ella peered deeper into the bowl, a little too close for my comfort.

"Good job your gran's not here then," I pointed out, shifting the mixer a little further away. "Even though this cake is absolutely fine." Hadn't Mac given her the master baker line?

"OK. Good."

Ella straightened up a bit, so she wasn't actually breathing down my neck any more, which was a bonus, but I could still feel how tense and stiff she was beside me. It was distracting.

"I do know what I'm doing here," I said, grabbing the vanilla.

Ella's eyes grew wide and apologetic. "I'm sure you do. Sorry. It's just … my gran makes the best Victoria sandwich in England. And…"

"You think she's going to critique your cake? Like, score you out of ten or something?"

I'd meant it sarcastically, but Ella nodded. "Oh, she absolutely would."

"But she won't be at the meeting, will she? So she won't get to taste it anyway."

Ella didn't look reassured – I didn't think she would until she had the finished cake in her hands – but she passed me the bowl of flour and didn't peer over my shoulder as I started to add it to the mixture, which was progress.

We were running behind after all our chatting. By the time I'd folded in the flour, the others already had their cakes in the oven. Yasmin and Grace were clearing up at their station, but Jasper and Mac left their mess for a moment and came to clutter up our space instead.

"What you doing?" Mac asked, elbows resting on the opposite side of the counter, so when I glanced up, his face was right in front of me, smirking. My heart jumped, surprised by his attention. I wasn't used to having that kind of focus on me. It felt weird. But kind of nice too.

I turned back to the scales. "I'm weighing the tins to make sure they each have an equal amount of cake mixture in." With four tins instead of two, it was harder to get them even. Harder still knowing it wasn't just my own obsessive tendencies we were dealing with here, but those of Ella's gran's Mothers' Union buddies too.

"Yeah, I got that. But why? We just bunged ours in when they looked about right."

"I noticed." I'd tried not to watch too closely how Mac and Jasper were getting on with their cakes, but from what I did see, they'd be lucky if they came out even enough to sit one on top of the other. "Weighing them makes sure they're equal, which means they'll cook evenly and match perfectly when it comes to making up the cake."

"Not if you don't get them in the oven soon," Jasper pointed out. "Miss Anderson is starting to look impatient…"

Ella bounced nervously beside me and I suppressed an eye roll, then checked the last tin again. "Don't worry. I'm done." Mac and I set them on the trays and carried them over to the ovens, shutting the doors carefully to make sure we didn't knock all the air out of the mixture.

When we got back, Jasper was already helping Ella clear our station, chatting away as he did so.

"Looks like you're with me," Mac said, and I had to stop my mouth curving up at the edges. It was washing up, not a date.

I followed him to his counter, surveying the chaos. "I can't decide if Jasper left to flirt with Ella or to avoid clearing up this mess. How did you manage to use every single mixing bowl?"

"Natural talent. And I don't think Jasper's up to flirting yet. I tried to give him some advice, but he got a bit freaked out at the idea."

Helping others again. Was it possible that Mac really was a nice guy under the too-cool-for-school attitude?

He tossed me a tea towel. "Come on. I'll wash, you dry."

"So how come you got Jasper to swap with Ella?" I asked, as Mac ran the water.

He shrugged. "Like I said. Her need was greater."

"Did she tell you about her gran's perfect cake obsession?"

"No." Mac's hands plunged into the bubbles, damp patches splashing up on to his shirt. "But she was tense as anything. Kept saying that the cake had to be perfect. That's how I knew she was an ideal partner for you."

He flashed a smile to show me he was joking, but I knew he wasn't. Not really. "Well, she drove me crazy with all the double-checking, but hopefully she'll get her perfect cake."

"She will," Mac said. "You're freakishly good at this."

A warm feeling flowed through me at his words, even if he had just used freakish as a compliment. I *was* good at this. And it felt great to be doing it again.

"I bet you practise a lot," he went on, handing me the next plate. Then he chuckled. "I can just imagine your kitchen. You keep everything in glass jars and label them, don't you? Like on TV. Go on, admit it."

"I might do." But thinking about my kitchen just

made me remember my dad singing along to the Rolling Stones while he kneaded bread, so I stopped. "And what about you? Do you even know where your kitchen is?"

Mac scrubbed out the bowl they'd used. "Sure. It's where my brother Jamie keeps the coffee. And his Rihanna calendar."

Shaking my head, I held out a hand for the mixing bowl. "Well, a few more weeks of Bake Club and maybe you'll develop an appreciation of a clean, well stocked kitchen."

The look Mac gave me suggested he didn't think it was very likely.

We waited around for the cakes to cool. Miss Anderson said we could take them home and build them there, but no one seemed particularly eager to leave, so she said she'd get on with some marking while we waited.

"My gran's cake usually has a creamy layer, as well as the jam," Ella said, peering at the picture accompanying the recipe.

"Buttercream," I answered promptly. "I've got the butter and icing sugar here; we can whip up a batch while we wait for the cakes to cool."

Jasper groaned. "I'm going to be washing the mixer again, aren't I?"

"Oh, could you!" Ella said, beaming at him.

Jasper's shy smile suggested the prospect of more washing up wasn't so bad if Ella was involved.

The boys wandered off while I got the mixer set up again and fished in my bag for butter and icing sugar.

"So ... Jasper." Ella bit her lip. "He's your year, right?"

I nodded. "Yeah. You're the only Year Ten, for some reason."

"There aren't many of us taking food tech in my year, either," Ella said. "But Bake Club is loads more fun. Guess your year was just more into cooking and baking."

"Uh, maybe." Or under more pressure from Mr Carroll.

Watching the butter carefully, I prepared the first spoon of icing sugar to add in once it was all nice and fluffy.

"Is, uh, Jasper taking food tech?"

"No." If he was, he'd have a better idea of what to do. But we didn't do a lot of straight baking in food tech, which I guessed was one of the reasons Miss Anderson had started Bake Club. And to let those students not studying food tech have a go, of course. "Why do you care?"

Ella turned bright red. "Well, I just wondered…
You're friends with him, right? I was just wondering
what sort of things he was into."

It looked like Jasper wasn't the only one with a
crush. "Why don't you ask him?" I suggested. Now
I wasn't just getting to know people, but turning
into a veritable matchmaker. This was definitely
progress.

Ella turned away. "Maybe another week. Once
Gran's feeling better. Or when Dad's back."

I guessed she needed to work up the courage.
I wouldn't rush her. Well, not today, anyway. "Does
your dad work away a lot?"

Ella looked a little relieved at the change of
subject. "He always has. Usually he's home a month
then away a month. Something like that. I spend a lot
of time at Gran's."

"Must be hard," I said. But to be honest, I was
thinking how much I'd give to have a dad who was
only home six months out of the year, instead of not
at all.

Ella gave me a look like she'd just remembered
the one thing she knew about me. "It's not so bad.
I mean, I've got my gran."

From what she'd told me, I wasn't sure how much
of a consolation that was. But Ella was still giving me

that pitying look I'd hated so much in the weeks after the funeral, so I turned back to the buttercream for a change of subject.

"I think this is ready," I said, switching off the mixer. "Want to check if the cakes are cool?"

They weren't stone cold, but Miss Anderson said that if any of us wanted to get home that night, they were going to have to do. As Ella and I prepared to spread our bottom layers with buttercream and strawberry jam, I was surprised to see Mac and Jasper also bringing a mixing bowl to the table.

"You made buttercream?" I asked, and Mac shrugged.

"He wanted to try it," he said, jerking a thumb in the direction of where Jasper was smearing a pale-coloured substance on his cake.

I frowned, peering into their bowl. "Um, what did you use?"

"You said butter and sugar," Mac replied.

"Icing sugar. I said icing sugar."

"Well, sugar is sugar isn't it? It did look a bit ... weird. So we added the other stuff we had left over."

"Other stuff?" I asked, trying not to wince.

"Flour. Eggs. That kind of thing."

I squeezed my eyes closed. "He's putting raw cake mix in his Victoria Sandwich."

"Guess so." When I opened my eyes, Mac was smirking. "But it tastes *incredible*."

Shaking my head, I turned back to my own, perfect cake, and the one for Ella's gran's friends. They were exactly equal; buttercream and jam precisely layered for effect. A small dusting of icing sugar and they'd be done.

Of course, Ella seemed much more interested in Jasper's potentially stomach-churning cake. She had her elbows resting on the counter beside him, watching engrossed as he spread cake mix over his sponge.

"Fine. But don't come crying to me when you get salmonella," I teased Mac.

He licked the cake mix off the spoon, smacking his lips. "I'll die happy," he said, holding the spoon out towards me and waggling it. "Go on. You know you want to."

I couldn't help myself. I laughed out loud and, bypassing the licked spoon, reached into the bowl for a taste of my own.

BLUEBERRY MUFFINS

1. Heat the oven to 190°C/fan 170°C/gas 5.
2. Sift together 225g of plain flour, 1 tsp of baking powder and 1 tsp of bicarbonate of soda.
3. Add 100g of caster sugar.
4. Stir in 125g of blueberries and the zest of 1 lemon.
5. In a jug, whisk together 1 large egg, 60g of cooled, melted butter, 150ml of milk and the juice of 1 lemon.
6. Add the egg mixture to the dry ingredients and stir together, until just combined.
7. Divide the mixture equally between muffin cases in a 12-hole muffin tray.
8. Bake for 15 to 20 minutes, until a cake tester or skewer comes out clean.

I'd managed to avoid my first meeting with Mrs Tyler, the school guidance counsellor, for almost two weeks, aided by a flu bug doing the rounds at school that laid her out. But now she was back and apparently eager to see me.

I didn't hurry out of my English lesson. The office we were meeting in was halfway across the school and if I took my time getting there, that meant less time being encouraged to share my deepest feelings with a stranger. Maybe I could claim I got lost ... but even that would only grant me a reprieve for this week. No, I needed a long-term strategy to deal with this woman.

I could just refuse to talk, but apparently that approach had run its course. If I appeared too unwilling to cooperate, they'd definitely call Mum in. Or worse, visit her at home.

There was the truth, but no way was I telling Mrs Tyler that. Besides, who ever really wanted to hear the truth? No, Mrs Tyler wanted to hear what she expected to hear – that I was withdrawn after my dad's death, but ready to make an effort to reconnect. And then she wanted to feel like she was helping me achieve that.

Which meant I needed to tell her about my efforts to fit in. Basically, Bake Club.

Too soon, I was outside Mrs Tyler's office. With a deep breath, I knocked on the door and pushed it open when she called for me to come in.

I wasn't sure what I'd been expecting from a guidance counsellor, but this wasn't it. With her permed red hair and oversized, navy-framed glasses, she looked like a throwback to one of the old films Mum liked to watch in the afternoons sometimes.

"Lottie," Mrs Tyler said, with a broad smile on her coral-painted lips. "Have a seat."

Her office was festooned with bluebirds. On every shelf, hanging from the blinds, even a framed poster of one on the back of her door. A fuzzy bluebird sat on the desk in front of me, and I couldn't help but stare at it.

"You spotted Happy, I see," Mrs Tyler said, sitting back down. "The bluebird of happiness. It always cheers me up."

Suddenly, I knew exactly how this was going to

go. Mrs Tyler wanted to make me *happy* again. God, working with teenagers must be like fighting gravity for her.

"That's nice," I said cautiously.

"But we're not here to talk about me, are we?" She folded her hands on the desk in front of her. "What makes *you* happy, Lottie?"

My mind went blank. "Um … doing a good job?" That sounded reasonable, right? Like I was a good student, trying to get back on track.

Mrs Tyler nodded. "What else?"

Now she was pushing. "Baking," I said firmly. Time to get on plan and remind her of all the things I was doing to fit in again at school.

"Like in Bake Club," Mrs Tyler said, and made a note on the pad in front of her. I tried to read it upside down, but she was using weird scribbles instead of actual words. Shorthand, I supposed. "That's good."

She put down her pen, slipped her glasses off her nose and stared at me, and I couldn't help but focus on her lilac eye shadow and the way it gathered in the creases of her lids.

"The most important thing you need to know about these meetings, Lottie, is that I'm here to listen to you. I want to learn about you. I want to help you learn about yourself."

"I think I know myself pretty well," I said, frowning.

Mrs Tyler's smile was faint. "Perhaps. But there's always more to find out, I promise you."

"So ... how do we start?" I wanted to get this over with as quickly as possible. And the sooner I knew what she wanted to hear, the sooner I could say it and get out.

"Why don't you tell me a little bit about your dad?" she said, sitting back to listen.

Inwardly, I gave a little sigh of relief. Yeah, talking about Dad brought back painful memories. But it was a hell of a lot better than talking about Mum.

Straightening up in my chair, I began to spin the tale of my perfect childhood and watched her lap it up.

On Wednesday, Mac showed up in my food technology GCSE class, proving once and for all the story about Mac having been kicked out of design tech. Rumour had it that he'd spent the last two weeks reading up on food safety and hygiene in Mr Carroll's office, before he was allowed to join in with the class. I didn't imagine they had much hope of Mac actually passing the GCSE, joining at this late stage, but they had to do something with him, and no one wanted to get food poisoning from being his partner.

He didn't sit beside me, of course, choosing instead to pair up with a girl I recognized as one of his mates' girlfriends. But he did flash me a quick grin as he walked past, before slouching into his seat and ignoring Miss Anderson for the next forty-five minutes.

I wanted to ask him about it when I got to Bake Club the next day, but he was already paired up with Ella again, leaving Jasper leaning against his counter looking miserable. I decided to view this as a challenge. I didn't like seeing Jasper looking so unhappy, and Ella was clearly interested, so all they needed was a little nudge. If it made them happy, I was sure Mrs Tyler would approve.

Across the room, Yasmin and Grace were pulling ingredients out of their wicker baskets, every inch the model bakers. It looked like Grace had decided that accessories were the key to being a great baker and had persuaded Yasmin too. So, Bake Club was going to be just like Drama Club, with Grace the perfectly outfitted star. After years of watching her land all the starring roles and then dealing with her snide comments the one year I got the junior lead, leaving Drama Club behind the year before had almost been a relief. I didn't really fancy a rerun.

But then, I didn't need a Little Red Riding Hood wicker basket to prove that I was a great baker. And I was happy out of that gang, making new friends. Like Jasper. Who, despite being labelled as a weird Goth kid, was actually kind of sweet.

Placing my bag of ingredients on the counter top, I pulled out the week's recipe. "Are you a blueberry muffin fan?" I asked Jasper, trying to distract him from mooning over Ella.

Jasper tore his gaze away from her to look at me. "They're OK. I prefer chocolate ones."

"Then you're in luck." I pulled out a punnet of raspberries and one of blueberries, waving them in front of his face. "I brought alternatives. And..." Reaching deeper into the basket, I found the packet I was looking for. "White chocolate chips to go with the raspberries."

Jasper's face lit up, for a second. "But we don't have a recipe for raspberry muffins."

I started laying out my ingredients in order. "Muffins are easy. Once you've got the basic mix down, you can add pretty much anything you like."

We started with the blueberry muffins, as a template. They were so quick, I knew we'd have time to make another batch. While they were in the oven, I measured out the ingredients for the raspberry and white chocolate ones, then turned to Jasper.

"Think you can manage this lot solo?"

His eyes widened. "Me? Alone?"

Time to put my "happy Jasper" plan into action. "Well, with Ella."

The eyes got bigger. He didn't need the eyeliner he added after school with fear like that. "She's working with Mac."

"She'll swap, I know it." Never mind Mrs Tyler. I wanted this for Jasper. I was already missing his puppyish joy.

"What if I screw it up?"

"Jasper, she couldn't take her eyes off you while you put raw cake mix in your Victoria sandwich last week. I'm sure however the muffins turn out, she'll love them."

He looked a little surprised to hear me speaking so bluntly. Strange how, after a year of avoiding people, I had fallen back into my old habits so easily. Maybe it was something about the food tech classroom that made me feel at home. Or maybe it was just time for me to be me again.

Jasper still looked nervous, so I decided to toss him in at the deep end. Walking over to Mac and Ella's station, I put on my best happy face and said, "Ella? Jasper's making raspberry and white chocolate muffins. He thought you might like to help…"

She glanced up at Mac for permission and he raised an eyebrow. "Go on. I'm sure I can manage a few measly muffins on my own."

"Well, I can help," I offered.

"In that case, I can probably make twenty-four muffins with the exact same number of blueberries in each one."

They weren't quite that even, but it came close.

"So, guys, the information pack came!" Miss Anderson shook a large envelope at us from the front of the class. I tried to focus on the clearing up instead, but her enthusiasm was kind of infectious, and it wasn't long before Mac and I found ourselves listening in too.

"There are three main competitions, all held on one very long day of baking in central London," she said, flipping through the brightly coloured booklet. "A group competition, a pairs one and an individual one."

"What will we have to bake?" Grace asked. She, at least, seemed enthusiastic about the idea.

"All sorts of things. There's a technical challenge, to be announced on the day. And you'll 'have the chance to show off your own recipes' too, it says."

"Like we have any of those," Mac murmured next to me.

I nodded. It did seem a little ambitious for a group who'd barely been baking a fortnight. Grace, Yasmin and I at least had our food tech knowledge, but Mac, Jasper and Ella were completely new to this.

Miss Anderson was obviously having the same thought. She placed the booklet on her desk and looked round the room at us. "There are leaflets here for you to take home and a parental consent form you'll need to get signed. But I want you each to read through the information for yourselves and think about whether you want to be involved. It's a big commitment and will take a lot of work. Baking for a couple of hours a week with me isn't going to be enough. You'll need to practise in your own time too. So think about it."

"What do you think?" Mac asked, as we all got stuck back into the clearing up.

"About the competition?" I considered. "I'm not sure. I mean … it could be fun. But…"

"It could be work too," Mac finished.

"Are you going to pick up a leaflet?"

Mac tilted his head to the side, considering. "May as well. Can't do any harm, I suppose."

"Yeah. I guess." Except for the part about

additional practice. On top of my coursework and revision and, more than anything, the ... situation at home, I had a feeling that might be impossible.

Mac tossed his tea towel into the hamper after drying his hands, snapping me out of my thoughts. "Same time next week," he said, and I smiled. That, at least, was something to look forward to.

From that week on, it was just assumed that Mac and I would work together, same as Grace and Yasmin. Jasper and Ella would flutter around each other at their workstation, jumping whenever their hands accidentally touched.

Over at our workstation, I'd measure the ingredients, ready for Mac to mix them. He'd do the washing-up and I'd dry. It was nice. It felt almost like a real friendship.

But our hands never seemed to accidentally touch at all.

Not that I cared.

Much.

That evening, tin of muffins tucked under my arm, I headed home, still grinning. My house wasn't far from the school, about a ten-minute walk, and hidden away in a little cul-de-sac off a bigger road.

Lots of people thought we'd move when Dad died.

73

But Dad's death-in-service payment had cleared the mortgage, and the life insurance and spouse's pension Mum got covered pretty much everything else, so there was no real reason to have to move. Besides, by the time Mum surfaced long enough from her fog of loss to even think about it ... well, we were already pretty stuck where we were.

So every single day I walked home past the spot where he died. Past the pavement where the crowd gathered round him after he'd rushed out of Walnut Crescent on to Orchard Avenue, where the speeding car didn't see him until it was far, far too late.

After a whole year, I'd almost grown used to it. I still remembered, every time, but these days it felt more like a way of being close to him than a reminder.

And I still liked looking out of my bedroom window at the back garden and the swing he'd built for me when I was five. Liked remembering him perched on my bed, reading *Alice in Wonderland* to me, one chapter a night, when I was six. Thought of him every time I looked into the kitchen and imagined us baking there together, in some impossible future.

I opened the front gate, took a deep breath as I reached the doorstep and put my key into the lock.

It took a few shoves to get the door open enough

to squeeze through. The doormat had long been lost under a sea of newspapers. I'd tried moving them once, but Mum was scared that we might miss something if we threw them out and there wasn't really anywhere else in the house for them to go.

When Dad was alive, Mum had kept our house like a show home. Show homes, in case you've never had the joy of trawling round them with your parents so your mum can get ideas, generally look very smart, but they're not exactly places you want to live. Like some designer had to come up with a version of cosy and welcoming that didn't involve any actual comfort, or any sign of the people who are actually meant to live there. No photos, no personalization, no soul.

That changed when Dad died. Suddenly Mum wanted something to remember him by, only there wasn't a whole lot that had survived her latest decluttering purge.

And so the recluttering started.

Wedging the door open with my shoulder, I manoeuvred my large tin of muffins inside, shuffling in behind it and letting the door close. I prepared myself by letting out a long breath then, finally, had to inhale again.

Our house used to smell of fresh air or expensive cinnamon-scented candles. Now it smelled of decay, mingled with overpowering cheap air fresheners that really didn't live up to their name. It was like dying roses, all the time, and sometimes, if I forgot to breathe through my mouth, I could feel the nausea rising up from my stomach at the stench of it.

"Lottie? Is that you?" Mum's voice floated down the stairs, over the stacks of magazines and books that lined the steps and the teetering piles of plastic food containers above them. They were, at least, all cleanly washed out – my contribution to our continued good health. The ones in the kitchen – the ones I couldn't reach because of the stack of crates full of heaven-only-knew-what that Mum had brought back from the charity shop the week before – I dreaded to think what was growing in there.

"Yeah, Mum. It's me." We went through this ritual every day. I didn't know who else she thought it might be; we hadn't had guests in the house since the wake. She'd stopped answering the door and even the phone, and eventually her friends had stopped calling altogether. Maybe it was just paranoia speaking. She wouldn't want anyone to see the house in such a state.

Of course she wouldn't throw out any of her junk, either – believe me, I'd asked. I'd begged. I'd pleaded. I'd tried getting rid of it when I thought she wouldn't notice, but she had a freakish ability to remember exactly what was where, even in the crazy House of Stuff.

"I brought blueberry muffins," I called up. Sometimes Mum would come out of her nest for food. I'd had to move the microwave and a mini-fridge into my bedroom a couple of weeks earlier, when the last of my secret passages through the Maze of Junk to the oven got blocked up by three boxes of *National Geographic* magazine back issues.

Dad had loved *National Geographic*. I hadn't had the heart to shout at Mum when she brought those home.

I heard the creaking of overstrained floorboards and Mum's thin face appeared at the top of the stairs. "Blueberry? I wish we had raspberry."

I couldn't tell her I'd given up the raspberry and white chocolate muffins to try and get Jasper a date, so I just looked up, apologetic. "Sorry. Only had blueberries today."

She sighed, "Oh well," and retreated into the shadows, the TV getting louder from inside her room. She'd be wrapped up in her blankets again. She tended to tuck them over her head, so she needed to turn the telly up to hear it better.

The blankets were probably due a wash. I'd have

to try and chase her out of the house at the weekend so I could clean them. Maybe even find a new path to the kitchen and clean in there.

Of course the downside of Mum being out of the house was that she raided the charity shops for more Stuff, wasting our savings on things we really didn't need.

"Someone just gave this away," she'd say when she returned, hugging the item to her chest. "All the precious memories it must hold … and they just gave it away." Then she'd shake her head and wander off to find a place to keep it.

Reaching into my bag, I pulled out a perfectly rounded blueberry muffin and took a bite. Maybe the sugar would help me come up with a plan to make sure that Mrs Tyler never saw the inside of our home.

A piece of paper fluttered to the floor, dislodged from my bag. I rescued it before it got lost in the sea of rubbish. The competition leaflet, of course.

I shoved it back in, pushing it down to the bottom. I'd never be able to bake in this house again, and there was no point pretending otherwise. Miss Anderson had said we'd have to practise outside the club, and I couldn't do that.

So what was the point?

PUMPKIN PIE

1. Heat the oven to 190°C/fan 170°C/gas 5.
2. In a large bowl combine 400g of pumpkin puree (use tinned pumpkin puree or make your own), 175g of caster sugar, 1 tsp of cinnamon, 1 tsp of ginger, ½ tsp of salt, ½ tsp of nutmeg and ¼ tsp of ground cloves.
3. Add 3 eggs and beat lightly until combined.
4. Gradually add 300ml of milk, stirring until combined.
5. Pour the filling into a pastry-case shell.
6. Bake for 1 hour, until a knife inserted near the centre comes out clean.

"This week, we're going to do something a little bit different," Miss Anderson said, as if we hadn't all noticed that already.

For one thing, we hadn't been asked to bring any ingredients for the club. "I'll take care of it," she had said the week before. Which meant I'd spent seven whole days wondering what on earth we'd be baking the following week. Didn't she know I hated surprises? Baking was supposed to be surprise-free.

But maybe that was just my bad mood talking. I'd been cross all week since my second session with Mrs Tyler, where she wrote far more notes than the first week, and said "Hmm" a lot. Nothing that had happened since had improved things. Certainly not finding Mum putting on her coat in the hallway on my way to school that morning, excited by her plans to visit a car boot sale. Apparently they were a great source of magazines. Because, of course, we didn't have nearly enough of them.

And that wouldn't be all. There'd be a few more precious memories she couldn't bear to see go to waste, even if the memories concerned weren't hers. More Stuff to cram into our already bulging house.

Just great.

But it turned out there was worse to come. Right before Bake Club, I'd stumbled across Mrs Tyler talking to Mr Carroll in the hallway. I'd hung back enough that they didn't see me, but not so much that I didn't hear Mrs Tyler say, "I really do think we need to talk to the mother."

I could still feel the panic rising inside me, but I tried to stamp it down as I listened to Miss Anderson. Maybe Mrs Tyler hadn't been talking about me. And if she had? I was in the best place to try and prove her wrong.

Bake Club didn't have piles of clutter or stacks of magazines. But it did have a pile of filled-in parental consent forms sitting on Miss Anderson's desk, and people chatting excitedly about a competition I knew I had no chance in. My form was still crumpled up in my bag. Unsigned.

Still, being there was better than being at home. So I sat up a little straighter on my stool, waiting for Miss Anderson's explanation and hoping that it would lift my bad mood.

Beside me, Mac had his cheek resting on his palm, his elbow planted halfway across the counter. I wanted to nudge him to attention, but I was afraid he might just fall off. Was he actually *asleep*?

Looked like I'd be listening for two, as usual.

"As you probably all noticed, I'm not from around here." Miss Anderson's American twang got stronger with the second half of the sentence and everyone giggled. Well, everyone except Mac, who looked about a blink away from snoring. "Back home, today is our holiday, Thanksgiving, which I imagine you've all heard of. And I thought it would be nice if we baked some traditional Thanksgiving dishes to share together and talked about all the things we're thankful for."

My understanding of Thanksgiving came entirely from American TV shows, but I was pretty sure it was the sort of thing you were supposed to do with your family, not a random selection of students you barely knew. But maybe Miss Anderson didn't have any family here to celebrate with. If we were the next best thing she could come up with, I supposed I didn't mind.

And anyway, I couldn't help but wonder what Mac was thankful for.

Miss Anderson placed a bag of ingredients on

each of our workstations and we dived in without waiting for an explanation.

"Since we only have limited time, I've given you each a few shortcuts, to make sure we have enough time to enjoy your creations at the end."

I pulled out a ready-made pie crust and a tin of pumpkin puree. Part of me was a little miffed that she didn't think I could make a shortcrust pastry in time, but this was far quicker. And the others would probably have freaked at the idea of making pastry so early in their baking careers.

Mac plucked the pie crust from my hand with a yawn. "This looks surprisingly easy."

"I suppose." Looking under little bags of spices, I found the recipe and started laying things out in order.

"Let me guess," Mac said, reading over my shoulder. "You wanted to do things the hard way."

"The proper way."

Mac rolled his eyes. "Yeah, well, this way we get to eat pie sooner. I'm not really seeing a downside."

Miss Anderson stopped by our counter, smiling gently. "I'm sure you two could have handled making the crust yourself but, to be honest, today is more about the eating than the baking! I hope you don't mind."

"Of course not," I said, even though I did still, a bit. Maybe that was just because I'd rather be baking than trying to think of things to be thankful for. Or maybe because I really didn't want to have to share those non-existent things with the group.

"You can always boil up your own pumpkin and make your own pastry when you get home!" Miss Anderson suggested enthusiastically. "And I hope you'll bring some pie in to share with me if you do. I'm sure it will be wonderful."

She was being kind. Paying me a compliment even. But the reminder of my own kitchen and the piles of containers and cardboard and junk, meant that my smile was a little weak in return. "If I have the chance, I will," I said. I wasn't ever going to get the chance. Not in my house.

As Miss Anderson wandered off to check on Jasper and Ella, Mac nudged me with his elbow. "What's up with you?"

I shifted out of reach, not wanting to catch his eye. "Me? Nothing. Apart from worrying that you might fall asleep face down in my pumpkin pie."

"Our pumpkin pie," Mac corrected me and grabbed the recipe. "Isn't pumpkin a vegetable? Is this going to taste like—"

"It's a very sweet vegetable," I interrupted, before

84

Miss Anderson heard him finish that thought out loud. "It'll taste good, I promise." Even in my foul mood, I couldn't help but feel a little happier at the memory of my dad telling me exactly the same thing. We'd made pumpkin pie together one year, after I insisted on growing a pumpkin in my tiny garden patch. I'd wrinkled my nose when he suggested the recipe and he'd laughed and promised me I'd like it.

I had, of course. Dad was always right about what I would like. Nobody knew me like he did. It was hard to imagine that anyone ever would.

Mac's jaw cracked as he let out another huge yawn, barely hidden behind his hand. "Seriously, why are you so tired today?" I asked.

Mac pressed his fists against his eyes, trying to wake up. "My brother had a party last night. Went on a little late, that's all."

A party. Of course. While I'd been trying to perfect my history essay in my bedroom and ignore the growing piles of magazines lining the landing outside, Mac had been partying with his older brother. There'd probably been girls and beer and loud music, with Mac right in the middle, loving it all.

As if I needed a reminder of why we could never be real friends. We were just way, way too different.

"Well, see if you can stay awake long enough to

make this, yeah? If you manage, it can be what *I'm* thankful for."

Mac stared at me for a moment, then shook his head. "You're in a really bad mood today. It's a lot less fun."

"I'm in a perfectly good mood," I snapped, realizing only too late that I might have said it a little loud.

When I looked up, Jasper and Ella were staring at me, and even Yasmin was sneaking glances over. Grace just shook her head.

Ignoring everyone, I set about making the pie. Mac was going to be no help today anyway. It was far easier to just get on with it myself.

Mac obviously agreed because it didn't take long for him to wander off towards Jasper and Ella's station and I could hear them murmuring to each other, probably about me and my bad mood.

Great. I couldn't exactly explain to them what the matter was — how scared I was that Mrs Tyler would insist on seeing Mum. I could only imagine what would happen if anyone realized the state of the place we were living in, but my imaginings weren't pretty. Bottom line? They could take me away. And crazy as Mum was, I'd already lost enough parents, thank you very much.

I tried to ignore the murmurs and focus on the pie, but I couldn't help glancing up from time to time. Jasper and Ella were making apple pie and Mac had been conned into peeling and chopping the apples. I eyed my tin of pumpkin puree with disgust and made a decision.

Dropping the recipe on to the counter, I headed out to the toilets. I'd be done with my pie ages before the others, anyway, so I could take a few minutes out to try and beat this bad mood. Maybe even think of something to be grateful for.

The bathrooms were cool, if smelly, and I ran some water over my wrists and hands, then splashed my face to try and calm down.

It had been a rubbish week and this was the last thing I needed. What was I thankful for? That I'd managed to get my mum to leave her room for tea last night. That she hadn't noticed yet that I'd installed a lock on my bedroom door, so she couldn't get in and fill it with her Stuff. That I wasn't at home right then, watching her sort through her piles of magazines, placing them in an order that only she understood and never, ever getting rid of any of them.

Get it together, Lottie. I took a breath, and reminded myself how much worse things could be. Yes, this week sucked. But being a cow to my new friends

87

wouldn't help convince Mrs Tyler that I was happy. I needed to focus and pretend that everything was fine again.

Checking my reflection in the mirror and hoping the pinkness faded from my cheeks quickly, I headed back. But when I reached the classroom, I paused behind the doorway just long enough to listen to what was going on in my absence. It's not paranoia if everyone really is talking about you and it's not really eavesdropping when they're doing it at full volume.

"Look, I told you, I've got no idea," Mac said.

"Are you sure? Did you say something, maybe?" Ella asked, sounding concerned. "She's normally so cheerful."

"I yawned! That was all."

"Maybe she's tired," Jasper said.

"Maybe she's crazy," Mac muttered, still loud enough for me to hear from my hiding place.

Heat flooded my face and I ducked my head again. I reminded myself that I was trying to shift my bad mood.

"She's just being a drama queen," Grace said. "Playing it up for attention. Ignore her, Mac."

"And you'd know all about drama queens, right?" Jasper said.

"You might want to try being a little bit kinder

to Lottie today." Miss Anderson's soft voice made me freeze. "It would have been her dad's birthday tomorrow."

How did she know that? I panicked a little and then realized Mrs Tyler must have told her. Maybe asked her to keep an eye on me. I'd just have to hope that Miss Anderson wouldn't report back on my bad mood and lose me happiness points.

And in the meantime, I had to suck it up and carry on.

With a deep breath, I walked back into the classroom, not even letting myself look over to my friends until I got to my workstation.

"Well, that makes more sense." Mac's voice was low and when I risked a glance up, I caught his eye and looked away quickly. I didn't want to see his pity.

Swallowing the lump that seemed to have formed in my throat, I got back to my pie, mixing in the spices and focusing on the warm, Christmassy smell. This was something to be thankful for – the way that baking could take away the realities of the world around me.

"Hey, Lottie…" Mac leaned against the opposite side of the counter, picking up an empty bag of spices and fiddling with the cord that pulled it closed.

I paused in my pie making, waiting for him to go

on, but he didn't. With a sigh, I turned to face him properly, looking up to meet his eyes.

He held my gaze for only a moment before, shifting his weight to his other foot, he glanced away. "Um, anything I can do to help?" he said finally. He sounded apologetic and I figured that was as close to an actual "sorry" as I was going to get.

Which hopefully meant that I didn't have to apologize for my bad mood, either.

"We're nearly done," I said, giving the filling one last stir. "You can hold the pastry shell still while I pour this in, if you like?"

He did as I asked without saying anything more and then carried the tray over for Miss Anderson to put in the oven, while I started getting things together to wash up.

Jasper, on his way to get his apple pie cooked, paused at our workstation. "Are you OK?"

I didn't even bother faking a happy face. "Just dandy." One of my dad's phrases – I'd almost forgotten that. Had I been so focused on Mum in the last year that he was starting to slip away from me?

I waited for Jasper to keep walking. Instead, he reached over and rested a hand on mine. "Just ... you know we're your friends, right? And we worry. So if you want to talk ... I've got fifteen years of parental psychobabble I can use."

"I'm OK," I said. "I don't want ... I don't *need* to talk about anything."

Jasper's eyes were serious as he nodded. "OK, then. But if you ever do..."

"Right. Sure." I bit my lip as he started to move away. "Jasper?" I called, and he turned back. I gave him an apologetic smile. "Thanks."

He smiled back. "Any time."

After washing up, Miss Anderson got us all to sit round the big table in the middle of the room, the scents of apple, pumpkin and pecan pies filling the air.

"Like I said, in my family," she said, smiling at the memory, "we always used to sit round the table together while we waited for my mum to bring out the pies. And we'd talk about all the things we were thankful for over the past year. So, I'll start."

I looked down at the table, my bad mood bubbling up again despite my intentions. It was all very well for Miss Anderson, with her classic American family traditions. It was easy to sit round and be thankful when you had a whole family and a mum who made fantastic pies. A little harder when your dad was dead and your mum had lost it.

I glanced at the others and wondered who else felt the same way. No one, probably. I bet Yasmin, with her beloved brothers and outsized family, had a whole list. And Grace, with her wealthy parents and huge, immaculate house. Even Jasper, whose parents were clearly a little crazy, knew that he always had their attention. Ella had her gran, who she obviously adored enough to fake a cake for, even if I thought she sounded a little scary.

And Mac. I didn't know about Mac. Maybe he had issues. The arson would certainly suggest so.

But none of the other Bake Club members looked particularly enthusiastic about sharing their thankfulness. In fact, none of them were looking up at all; every one of them just stared at the table.

"This year, I'm really thankful I found such a great group of students to be part of my Bake Club," Miss Anderson said.

I wanted to roll my eyes, to mutter about how clichéd or stupid that was. But she said it so honestly, beaming at us all, it was hard to be cynical.

Yasmin, sitting on her left, went next. "Um, I guess I'm thankful for my family. Especially having my brother back home safe from the army, with his wife and kids." She gave us a half-smile. "And I'm grateful that being in Bake Club lets me escape the craziness of my full house for a few hours a week."

Ella went next, predictably being thankful for her gran, and that her dad was coming home the next week. Jasper, it turned out, was mostly grateful his parents were off at a conference that weekend, so he might get some peace and quiet with only his cousin staying to keep an eye on him.

Grace went next, and I couldn't help but predict what she might be thankful for. Blond hair dye? Finally filling out that bra she'd made her mum buy her in Year Seven and told everyone about? Resentful, mean thoughts, to suit my mood.

Then Grace said, "I'm grateful for my friends, especially the ones I've made at Bake Club." She smiled at Yasmin as she spoke, but her arm rested right next to Mac's, touching his as she turned her gaze on him.

Mac didn't even look at her as he moved his arm casually out of reach. I didn't bother trying to hide my smirk.

"Mac," Miss Anderson said. "What about you? What are you thankful for this year?"

Mac's smile was crooked as he stared straight at me. "I'm just thankful that Lottie knows how to bake."

I blushed as the others laughed, all except Grace. But I didn't need her to. I had the others now, didn't I? Maybe they still talked about me behind my back, but they talked *to* me too. And that was new.

"Fair enough," Miss Anderson said, smiling. "And Lottie?"

I couldn't think of anything. My mind went utterly blank. What was there in my cluttered and confusing life to give thanks for?

Looking around the room for inspiration, I shrugged. "I guess … I suppose I'm just thankful I joined Bake Club."

The timer on the oven pinged, distracting everyone from my admission and I hurried over with Miss Anderson to check on the pies. We served them up hot, and Jasper burned his tongue on the apple filling, and made us all laugh by jumping round the classroom waving his hands in front of his mouth. Even Grace giggled.

Mac leaned across the empty stool between us and nudged me gently. "Feeling better?"

Looking into his eyes I noticed he didn't look tired any more. They were wide and blue and watchful, as if he was taking in every bit of me, looking for signs I might be about to snap at him.

And just like that, the last wisps of my bad mood

evaporated. "I'm fine. How's the pie?"

Mac glanced down at the bowl in front of him and scooped a spoonful of the pumpkin pie into his mouth. As he chewed, his eyes grew even wider. "Incredible," he said, through a mouthful of crumbs.

Behind him, Jasper stumbled past again, Ella chasing him with a glass of water, Yasmin and Grace doubled over with laughter at the sight of them.

Watching the antics of my new friends, I realized I hadn't been lying about what I was thankful for. Bake Club had given me more than I'd ever expected it could. Even if it couldn't give me a chance of winning the competition. Maybe it was worth taking part, anyway. Just for the fun of it.

Making sure no one was looking, I pulled the parental consent form out from my bag, and scribbled Mum's signature across the bottom. She'd never know, and I wasn't going to let her obsession take this opportunity away from me. Slipping the form into the middle of the pile on Miss Anderson's desk, I felt a weight lift from my shoulders. The decision was made. I'd just have to figure out the practising thing somehow.

WHITE BREAD

1. Put 500g of strong white flour with 2 tsp of salt in a large mixing bowl.
2. Add a 7g sachet of fast-action dried yeast and mix.
3. Make a well in the centre and pour in 300ml of lukewarm water mixed with 2 tbsp of olive oil.
4. Mix to a soft dough, then turn out on to a lightly floured worktop and knead thoroughly for ten minutes.
5. Oil a 900g loaf tin and place dough inside.
6. Cover and leave to rise for 1 hour.
7. Heat the oven to 200°C/fan 180°C/gas 6.
8. Slash the top of the loaf with a sharp knife, then bake for 30 to 35 minutes, until risen and golden.
9. Tip out on to a cooling rack and tap the bottom of the loaf. If it sounds hollow, it's cooked.
10. Leave to cool for a few hours before eating.

There were a lot of rumours floating around school the next week. I only heard snatches – possible half-truths and probably lies. That Mac had left. That he'd been arrested. That he'd been expelled. I even heard someone claim he'd eloped with an older woman. I spent a lot of time reminding myself that rumours weren't the truth. But even more time scanning the yard outside the canteen for a glimpse of his dark hair, my heart sinking every time I thought I caught sight of him, only to realize it wasn't.

Something was definitely going on. Mac wasn't in food tech, either, or many other classes, as far as I could tell from asking around.

"Have you even seen him this week?" I asked Jasper, grabbing him outside the canteen at lunchtime on Wednesday. In the last few weeks, I'd come to know his routine, where to find him when. In fact, I'd found myself hanging out with Jasper quite a bit.

But Jasper shook his head. "Not sure anyone has.

He definitely wasn't in geography this morning."

"Maybe he's sick," I suggested.

"Or he's been expelled."

I gave Jasper a fierce look. "Not helpful."

"Yeah. We'd have seen teachers dancing in the hallways already, I'm sure." He glanced at me sideways. "You seem very concerned."

"He's my Bake Club partner."

"He's your friend," Jasper countered.

"Maybe." Was he? We barely spoke outside of Bake Club, and I still wasn't sure if that was because he was embarrassed to be seen with me. But when I'd been angry, he'd worried about me, and he was sweet to me, in his way. Perhaps we were friends.

I hoped so.

Jasper, I'd discovered over the last few weeks, had an astonishing nose for gossip. Maybe it came from his parents always wanting to know and understand everything about his life. But whatever it was, Jasper always knew the right questions to ask, and who to ask them. And in this case, it turned out, he hadn't even needed to go ferreting for details. He'd been right there.

"OK, so I don't know why he's not here this week, not really," he said. "But … you know there was a party last Friday night?"

"Grace's birthday party." Everyone in school knew about that party. I hadn't been invited, obviously. Not that I cared. But I hadn't realized that Jasper had. "You were there?"

He gave a brief nod. "We all were... Sorry."

I shouldn't be surprised. Not really. Grace wanted to be queen of Bake Club, same as she was queen of Drama Club. Which meant winning over her subjects. Of course she'd invite them. And why would she invite me? Hadn't I made it perfectly obvious that I didn't want to be part of school life any more? Bake Club was an exception to the rule. Besides, Grace didn't like competition, and I was a better baker than her. That was all.

Except I got an uneasy sort of feeling in my stomach at the thought of being left out.

"Mac was there?" I asked.

"Yeah. We were kind of surprised he showed up, actually."

"I thought if there was a party, it was a given Mac would be there." Wasn't that his reputation, after all? St Mary's wild child party boy. And I had first-hand proof – he'd been exhausted after his brother's party the week before.

"I guess. But I didn't think he and Grace were close. And..." Jasper trailed off and smiled at me.

I narrowed my eyes. "And what?"

"When Grace asked him, he wanted to know if you were coming. When she said you couldn't make it … he said he probably wouldn't be able to, either."

Something warm and tingly rose up inside my chest. He'd wanted to know if I would be there. Maybe he wasn't too embarrassed to be seen with me, after all.

"She said I couldn't go?"

Jasper shifted a little uncomfortably. "Yeah. She didn't invite you?"

"Doesn't matter. I probably *couldn't* have gone anyway." All that hiding alone in my room I had to do. Kept a girl busy. "So what happened at the party?"

Jasper rolled his eyes, and flicked his hair out of his face. "What usually happens at parties. The sixth formers smuggled in whisky and got sick drunk in Grace's parents' en suite. The neighbours complained because the music was too loud, then eventually threatened to call the police around midnight. We all scarpered before they got the chance. And Mac…"

"Yes?" Because this was the part I cared about. Someone was always going to get drunk, and I was never going to be invited to one of those parties, Grace's or anyone else's, so it didn't matter to me if the police got called. But something was going on with Mac, and I wanted to know what it was.

Jasper rubbed a hand over his forehead. "I'm not sure. There was something going on with him that evening, is all. He showed up in a foul mood and ignored the Bake Club lot – even Grace – to hang out with the sixth formers."

"And then?" I asked, trying not to sound as anxious as I felt. "Some people are saying that he got into a fight with some gang from across town. One against fifteen. Is it true?"

Jasper paused dramatically for a moment, before shaking his head. "Nah."

The tightness in my throat eased a bit, and I whacked him on the arm with my school bag. "So what happened? Tell me."

Jasper rubbed at his arm. "You're no fun today. OK, so it was kind of hot inside, and loud, and so I snuck outside for a bit, yeah?" He looked a little shifty as he said this, his eyes darting away from mine.

"OK. What then?"

"I saw Mac's brother, Jamie." Jamie had been in Year Eleven when we were in Year Seven, but I think we probably all remembered him. He'd been more notorious than Mac, in some ways. For a start Mac had never filled the canteen with stray dogs overnight.

Jasper's face turned serious. "He was there for Mac. Jamie told him their dad was looking for him, that he'd better get back. Mac argued, for a bit. But then Jamie's phone rang, and I could practically hear the yelling down the phone line from where I was hiding by the front door."

"So Mac went home with his brother."

"Yep."

I frowned. "There was no fight?"

Jasper winced. "There was no gang. As for the fight..."

"What happened?" I asked again, more resigned this time.

"Jamie was having a go at Mac. Saying he was sick of covering for him. That he didn't get why school was suddenly so important. And Mac ... he lost it a bit. Swung at Jamie."

"And Jamie swung back," I guessed. My jaw clenched at the thought of it. It was his own stupid fault, hitting his brother in the first place. But all I could think was, *Is he all right?*

"Yeah. Pretty hard, by the look of things. But after that he pulled Mac up and took him home. Said something like, 'You know it's not worth it.'"

"What's not worth it?" I asked, confused.

"Didn't say." Jasper pushed away from the wall.

"Jamie said, 'Just give him a couple of days and he'll forget all about you again.'"

"His dad, do you think?" What had Mac done this time that he needed his dad to forget? How bad was it?

"No idea. But that's what happened."

"Do you think he's OK?"

"What do I know? I mean, his dad sounded pretty mad, yeah. But Jamie didn't look like he was going to start beating Mac up again or anything. He's probably fine."

And he probably was, I tried to convince myself. Probably just too busy having fun, or slacking off to come to school, right? That was all.

Except I didn't believe it. Not really.

The next day, Bake Club day, I finally saw Mac again, and some of the tension I'd felt faded.

He was ducking into the hallway towards the food tech classroom, right at the start of lunch. I paused for a moment outside the main door, standing back to let out another stream of kids heading for the canteen, wondering if I should follow him. We weren't friends, not proper "tell each other everything" friends, whatever Jasper said. But if he was in the Bake Club room...

That was the one place we were partners. The one place I could ask him what happened, and where he'd been.

So I followed.

By the time I reached the classroom, the door had already swung shut behind Mac. It took a little deep breathing to get the courage to push it open again. He'd been scowling above his split lip and I had no illusions that he was the kind of person who took well to being asked questions about his personal life.

But I wanted to be friends, and this was what friends did, wasn't it?

I stood in the open doorway and blinked at the sight of Mac hauling a bag of flour out of his school bag, followed by a sachet of yeast.

He thumped them both down on the counter, then said, without looking up, "If you're coming in, I expect you to help me with this."

Dropping my bag to the floor, I let the door shut behind me. "I can do that."

"Good." Mac stared at the yeast. Now I was closer, I could see the purpling bruises fading round his left eye. Jamie really had got a good shot in. "Because I have no idea what I'm doing here."

"What are you making?" I also wanted to ask why.

What had made him take up baking in his lunch hour as well as after school? But I figured that question could wait until he wasn't giving his ingredients the death stare.

"Bread." Mac spat the word out. "Bog standard, boring bread. The sort you can buy anywhere. Explain to me why anyone would bother to make their own bread?"

He looked up at me for the last part, as if he actually expected an answer, so I said, "It tastes better than the shop-bought stuff."

"You've done this before, then? Of course you have. You've baked everything." He turned to the sink to wash his hands.

"I used to watch my dad do it," I corrected him. "But I think I remember."

"Good. You can be in charge of the recipe. Miss Anderson says I have to do the first part now to have it ready to bake tonight."

I nodded. "It'll need to rise this afternoon."

"Whatever. What do I do first?"

Grabbing the recipe card from the counter I scanned it quickly. A basic, easy bread recipe. I'd assumed we weren't doing bread because there wasn't the time to make it in an after-school club. But apparently Mac was a special case.

"Weigh out the flour," I instructed. "Five hundred grams."

"Right." Slamming the bowl down on top of the scales, Mac proceeded to dump the flour out into it in one heavy lot. "Damn. Too much."

My fingers itched to take over and do it right. "Want me to—"

"No." He didn't look at me, but there was a hint of a snarl in his voice. "I can do this myself."

I stepped back. "Fine. OK, then."

Carefully, Mac spooned flour back into the bag until the scales read exactly five hundred. "What next?"

"Um, add one sachet of the yeast and two teaspoons of salt."

He managed that without bother, and in turn I managed not to flinch too much when he tipped the whole jug of water straight into the flour, instead of gradually as the recipe said. Still, he stirred it and it came together in a dough OK, so I couldn't complain too much.

"Now you need to knead it."

Mac gave me a baffled look. "I need to *need* it?"

"Knead. With a K." Washing my hands, I sprinkled some flour on the surface and held my hand out for the bowl. "Don't worry. Given your practice as the human mixer, this should be easy."

I tipped the dough on to the flour, dusted my hands, and began to knead the dough, pushing it away from me, then pulling it back over itself, turning it by ninety degrees every now and then.

"My turn," Mac said, and I stepped aside without complaint. Kneading is hard work.

I rinsed my hands clean, then leaned against the counter to watch him work. The way the dough moved, the muscles in his forearms tightening and releasing ... it was strangely hypnotic. And the silence as he worked almost made me forget why I'd followed him in the first place.

But not quite.

"So ... I've heard a lot of stories about you this week," I said, my eyes drawn again to the purple bruise round his eye that had turned a sickly yellow colour at the edges.

Mac didn't look up from the dough. "Anything good?"

"The one about you eloping with a teacher was quite entertaining."

He snorted a laugh. "That the best they could come up with?"

"Is the truth any better?"

The dough slapped against the counter as he

turned it, more violently than before. "Is it ever?"

"I don't know. Want to tell me? I can judge."

Sighing, Mac shoved the heel of his hand into the dough again. "You're the pestering sort, aren't you? The sort that keeps asking."

I shrugged. "It's a new thing I'm trying. Getting to know people."

"Starting with me?"

"You were convenient."

The look he gave me was disbelieving, but I ignored it. "So what do you want to know?"

"Where you've been this week, I guess. Jasper said…" I trailed off, remembering that Jasper had been hiding at the party. Mac wouldn't have known he was being watched.

"Jasper. Of course." Mac shook his head and his hair ruffled and resettled in its usual curls. He had flour in it, I noticed, which gave him premature grey streaks. Maybe that was why he looked so much older than me right then. More world-weary.

"He's a gossip," I agreed. "He said he, well, heard that you left the party on Friday with your brother and no one had seen you since. He said… He said Jamie was pretty mad."

"Mad enough to punch me, you mean," Mac said. "Don't worry, I hit him first."

"So I heard."

He raised an eyebrow at me. "You don't approve?"

I didn't. But that wasn't the point. "I just don't understand what made you so mad. Or where you've been this week."

Mac slapped the dough down again. "I was working."

"At your dad's garage?" I asked, thinking back to our earlier conversation. "Because… Was he mad about the party?" I couldn't find a way to make sense of it in my head. If his dad was mad he'd gone out to a party, surely Mac would be in trouble a lot more often. But why had he sent Jamie to get him, otherwise? And why keep him out of school? Surely even Mac's dad thought school was more important than punishment. Hell, from what I'd seen, school practically was punishment for Mac.

But Mac laughed, a bitter bark of a sound. "No. Not because of the party."

"Then what?"

He sagged slightly, pushing at the dough with less force. "He found the competition leaflet and form in my bag. And then he asked around, found out I was swapping out my Thursday shifts with one of the other lads and skipping rugby on a Monday to make it up."

"It took him this long to work it out?" I asked. "I mean, so he was mad you've been missing rugby for Bake Club?"

"He's not usually around by late afternoon. Jamie runs the garage from three onwards. And it's not the rugby he's mad about."

But if it wasn't the rugby... "It's the baking," I said, finally catching on.

"You got it. Dad's a bloke's bloke. Not taking shifts at the garage for sport was one thing. But cakes? No way."

"Did you tell him you're only doing it because the school said you had to?"

"You think he listened long enough for me to explain?" Mac shook his head. "Wasn't worth the effort. I told Jamie, though. Then I worked off Dad's anger by going full-time at the garage for a few days this week. Chances are I can go right back to Bake Club without him even noticing. Jamie won't say anything unless he has to. And I can forge Dad's signature on the form easy enough. Not like I haven't done it before."

Something else we had in common that I couldn't tell him about.

"Didn't the school have a problem with you skipping three days because your dad was mad?"

How come they didn't notice Mac not even showing up, but I got threatened with the social workers for dropping Drama Club?

Mac just kept on kneading. "Jamie called and told them I was ill. Let's face it, no one's really concerned about my work slipping. Not much lower for it to go. They're all just waiting to kick me out at the end of this year, all the way over to the vocational college across town."

"Miss Anderson obviously cared," I said, nodding at the bread.

Mac pulled a face. "Yeah, well. She's new and enthusiastic. She told me that if I wanted to take part in the competition, I had to come and make this today."

He shoved the dough particularly hard on "this".

"Miss Anderson said that?" I asked, surprised. She always seemed like one of those teachers who cared more about being friends with her students than punishing them. Apparently she had her limits.

Mac gave a jerky, impatient nod. "I have to get my behaviour up to scratch, blah, blah, pass some mocks, the usual rubbish. If I want to stay in Bake Club, that is."

"And you want to stay in." It wasn't a question. There was something about Bake Club that he didn't want to let go of, not yet. I didn't pretend that it might be me.

"We're making Christmas cookies next week," Mac replied. "I love Christmas cookies."

But that wasn't all, I was sure. In fact, I was starting to suspect that Mac actually *liked* baking. For all his grumbling, he wanted to be part of Bake Club, even if he wouldn't admit it. And so, I realized, did I. Bake Club was the first thing that had meant anything to me since Dad died. I wanted to bake, wanted to take part, wanted to compete – wanted to win. Mac did too, and he couldn't practise at home, either. Something else we had in common.

"This done?" Mac asked, slinging the dough back down on the counter. "My arms are starting to ache."

I smiled. He might sound like he was complaining, but I knew better now. He could have skipped out on this, and missed the competition, but he hadn't.

Glancing up at the clock, I realized there wasn't a lot of lunchtime left. I couldn't remember quite when he'd started kneading, but he'd certainly done more than the ten minutes it said in the recipe.

"Yeah, think so," I said. Handing him the loaf tin I'd greased while he was working, I added, "We just need to cover it and let it rise. By the time we get back here after school, it'll be ready to bake."

"Great." He turned to look at me, but his gaze darted away almost immediately. "Look, Lottie…" he started, and suddenly there was a new tension in the air.

"I won't tell anyone," I said, guessing what was on his mind. "The elopement story's better anyway."

"OK. Thanks." He looked up at me again, his blue eyes serious, and for a moment I thought he was going to ask me something else. But then he waved a hand towards the loaf. "This better taste as good as you promised, you know."

"Was I wrong about the pumpkin pie?"

"No."

"Then trust me on this one."

He gave me a lopsided smile. "I guess I can do that."

We cleared up in comfortable silence, ready for the next class to come in. And when the bell rang, Mac walked with me across the yard towards my history classroom, before heading off for whatever lesson he had next.

For once, I didn't mind the people whispering as I went past. At least, until I saw Mr Carroll watching, his forehead furrowed. I looked away, pretending I hadn't noticed.

Hadn't he said he wanted me to make friends?

CHRISTMAS COOKIES

1. *Mix together 140g of sieved icing sugar, 1 tsp of vanilla extract, 1 egg yolk and 250g of soft, cubed butter.*

2. *Sieve in 375g of plain flour and mix to make a firm dough.*

3. *Split the dough in half and wrap each half in clingfilm, then chill for 30 minutes.*

4. *Heat the oven to 190°C/fan 170°C/gas 5.*

5. *Roll out the dough on a floured surface to about 1cm thickness.*

6. *Use Christmassy cutters to cut out your cookie shapes.*

7. *Place on lined and greased baking sheets, and use a skewer to make a 1-cm hole at the top of each cookie, for threading ribbon to hang them later.*

8. *Bake for 10 to 12 minutes until they're a light gold colour, then remove to cool on a wire rack.*

9. *For the icing, mix 200g of icing sugar with a few drops of cold water to make a thick but runny icing and colour with edible food colouring.*

10. *Spread the icing over the cooled cookies, decorate and thread with ribbon when set.*

"OK, this is not in any way what I signed up for." Mac's eyes widened as he took in the crowd of chattering Year Sevens occupying our food technology classroom.

"What are we supposed to do with them?" Grace asked, wrinkling up her nose.

"Maybe Miss Anderson just decided that even the Year Sevens have to be better at this than us," Jasper said. "Lottie excluded."

"Maybe we're supposed to teach them," I suggested, which earned me a collection of dirty looks.

"We should wait for Miss Anderson to tell us what we're doing today." Yasmin looked less nervous than the rest of us at the idea of spending our after-school time looking after a bunch of Year Sevens, but from what she'd told us about her brother's kids, it wasn't all that different from being at home for her.

Only Ella said nothing. Glancing over at her, I wasn't sure she'd even noticed the new additions to the classroom. Her pale skin had new undertones of greyish white, and her lip was caught between her teeth as she stared into the middle distance.

I nudged Jasper. "What's the matter with Ella?"

"No idea," he said, not looking. "She hasn't really spoken to me since the party."

Which was news to me. I'd thought Jasper and Ella had been getting pretty close. Although, now I thought about it, they had been a bit quiet at Bake Club last week. I'd been too preoccupied with Mac and his bread-tasting to really pay them much attention.

Before I could ask more questions, however, Miss Anderson finally arrived, looking a little flustered. Wispy strands of hair were escaping from her ponytail, and icing sugar dotted her top.

"Sorry to keep you guys waiting," she said, smiling. "But I promise, it's going to be worth it."

We must have all looked a bit sceptical, because she laughed. "OK, here's the plan. Year Seven need to make and sell Christmas cookies at the Christmas fair tomorrow, and we're going to help them. The Parents' Association have provided all the ingredients and decorations we need, so all we have to do is bake!"

"Why, exactly?" asked Jasper.

"Because it's a kind, community-focused thing to do. And because it will look good on our competition application form. Now, it's quite a big group, so we're going to do this in sections."

Putting a large basket on the workstation Mac and I had claimed as our own, she said, "This will be the baking station. Lottie and Mac will help the first group to actually make the cookie dough, then that group will move on to the next station –" a second bag landed on the next counter with a metallic rattle – "where they will cut out and bake the cookies with Jasper and Ella."

Some of the kids were eyeing Jasper with interest as he took up his station, presumably at the way he dug into the bag to pull out a Christmas tree cutter and waved it around wildly. Ella followed, standing beside him silently, hands clasped in front of her.

"I've got some dough I've already made up for group two to start off with," Miss Anderson said. "And once the cookies are in the oven, we move on to the decorating station, where Grace and Yasmin are in charge of icing, silver balls and edible glitter."

Grace beamed at the younger kids as she took up her station. Of course making things pretty would be her favourite task.

"Again, I've made some cookies ready for you to start with," Miss Anderson went on. "But by the end of the afternoon, everyone should have had a go at all three stations. So, Year Seven, line up and I'll split you into your groups."

While the Year Sevens were organized, us Bake Club members set about getting ready for them. Mac emptied the bag one item at a time, handing ingredients to me so I could put them in order.

"Ready?" Mac asked, and I looked up to see six eleven year olds making their way towards us, all in matching aprons.

"As I'll ever be," I replied, wiping my hands on my own apron and reminding myself it was all for the competition application. Our odds of winning might be slim, especially since Mac and I could only bake once a week at Bake Club. But still … I wanted the chance.

I felt the slight pressure of a hand against my back and Mac said, "You'll be great."

Whether the smile that formed on my lips was from his nearness or his words, I couldn't be sure. Either way, I was determined to prove him right.

It didn't take long to get everyone set up with bowls. We got the Year Sevens to take turns with the scales, adding each ingredient in turn. Then, of course, came the mixing. The butter we were using was soft and squidgy and I'd cut the cubes as small as I could, but it still took some arm strength to get everything combined into a nice, smooth dough.

Fortunately, we had Mac on our side. Every time one of the girls started to slow down, or dropped the spoon into the bowl to shake out her arm, Mac was on hand to help out. The boys, in an attempt to compete, insisted on doing it themselves, but by the time we reached the third group, the girls had given up even trying, preferring to watch Mac mix the dough instead. I didn't blame them. It was amazing how good a guy could look with a mixing bowl and wooden spoon in hand.

Soon the air was rich with sugar and vanilla, along with the chatter and laughter of the unusually full classroom.

"No, no!" I heard Jasper saying. "You need to do it with a flourish!" When I glanced over, he was wielding a stocking-shaped cutter with gusto, raising it in an arc above his head before bringing it down to the dough. Beside him, Ella stared resolutely at the dough on her half of the counter, whilst the kids got on with cutting out snowmen shapes.

Was Jasper acting up to try and get her attention? If so, it wasn't working.

Things were pretty manic, trying to get three lots of cookies made, baked and decorated in our limited after-school time, and by the time the Year Sevens were stripping off their aprons and queuing up to wash dough and icing and glitter from their hands, I, for one, was exhausted. Even Mac leaned against the counter in silence, massaging his mixing arm with his other hand. Standing next to him, I stared blankly at the movement for a moment before I realized and snapped myself out of it.

Finally, Miss Anderson took the Year Sevens out to find their parents. Mac wandered off in the direction of Grace and Yasmin's station, muttering something about looking for any broken biscuits that needed eating, and I took the opportunity to stop by Jasper and Ella's, to see if I could find out what was going on.

Jasper's previous enthusiasm seemed to have drained out of him and Ella looked even more glum than before. As I watched, I saw Jasper reach out to her, only for her to pull away.

"Well, that was fun!" I grinned brightly at them both, but got nothing approaching a smile in return. "Everything OK over here?"

"Who knows?" Jasper said, tossing the tea towel he'd been using to dry his hands on to the counter. "Somebody doesn't want to talk about it."

Even as Jasper glared at her, I saw Ella's eyes water, then she squeezed them closed a few times. Oh God, tears. I wasn't particularly good at tears.

But I had to be better than Jasper with the mood he was in.

I jerked my head towards the icing sugar and glitter station, trying to hint to Jasper that he should leave Ella to me for a while. His eyes narrowed as he tried to figure it out, but he got there in the end, skulking off towards Mac.

Perching on one of the stools, I watched Ella as she turned away from me, busying herself with a cloth and an already-clean patch of surface.

"He means well, you know," I said. "Jasper. He just... Well, he likes to know what's going on. Likes to understand people. I think it's genetic. Anyway, he only wants to help." Still Ella didn't look up. "But I know he can be kind of ... intense. And maybe you don't want to talk about whatever's the matter today. Which is fine too. But if you did..."

Still nothing. And Miss Anderson would be back soon. Time to try a new line of questioning.

"Did something happen at Grace's party? Jasper's been silent on the subject. Did he do something? Because I could talk to him, if you wanted—"

"Lottie. Just ... stop." Ella clenched her cloth, then dropped it and turned to face me at last. "It's not Jasper. I mean, yes, there was the thing at the party. But that's not… I'm not…" She trailed off, a tear escaping down her cheek. She shook her head. "I'm fine."

I knew all about saying "fine" when the world was falling apart. "You're really not. Look, you don't have to tell me. But if I can help at all…"

"Would you?" Ella looked up, eyes wide. "No. You can't."

As she shook her head and looked away, I resisted the urge to shake her. "Look, we want to help, if we can. We're your friends. So tell us what you need before Miss Anderson gets back."

Chewing her lip, Ella just stared at me for a moment, then gave a sharp nod, as if she'd come to a decision. "It's my gran."

"She's still sick?"

"She's … worse. And Dad called last night to say that his business trip's going to have to go on longer than planned."

"OK. What do you need us to do? Help look after her? Bake another cake?"

"Mince pies," Ella said glumly.

"Mince pies?" That didn't sound too bad.

"For the church Christmas fair. A hundred and fifty of them."

"Ah."

"Yeah. Gran promised and she'd so hate to let

them down. But she just can't do it herself. And neither can I."

"We're going to need the others' help."

Ella didn't look convinced, but she didn't argue either, so I turned to motion the others over. Jasper and Mac were already watching, and they came over without me having to say anything at all. Yasmin and Grace followed behind, looking curious.

"What's going on?" Mac asked, as Jasper made a beeline for Ella's side.

"Ella needs our help," I said. "We need to bake a hundred and fifty mince pies for her church Christmas fair on..." I glanced over at Ella.

"Sunday," she said, sounding miserable.

I winced. "Sunday. This weekend."

"Why, exactly?" Grace asked, one eyebrow raised.

"Because Ella's gran is ill and can't make them herself."

"So?"

Jasper glared at Grace. "What do you mean, so? Ella's our friend, so we are going to help her."

Grace tutted impatiently. "I mean, why can't Ella's gran just tell the church people she can't do it this year? Why can't Ella?"

I glanced over at Ella, who looked like she was about to fall apart. Jasper hovered nervously at her elbow, obviously unsure whether giving her a hug would help or make things much, much worse.

"Are you guys OK in here?" Miss Anderson called from the doorway, and we all turned towards her, shielding Ella behind our backs.

"Fine," Yasmin called out, quicker than the rest of us. "Just about to start clearing up, miss."

"Great, I just need to check in with the parents and staff setting up in the hall for the fete tomorrow. I'll be back in a few minutes." Miss Anderson wandered off again.

"So," I said. "Will you all help?"

"Of course," Jasper said, inching closer to Ella again. "Of course we will."

Yasmin moved a little closer, too. "I'm in. But where are we going to make them? I'm not sure Miss Anderson will let us take over the classroom tomorrow night."

"Miss Anderson can't know!" Ella snapped, her eyes back in their wide, frightened rabbit state. "She'd ask questions."

I frowned. What sort of questions was Ella afraid of? What did it matter if people knew we were helping Ella's gran out? But before I could ask, Mac said, "What about your place, Lottie?" A sense of dread crept through me. "Bet you've got all the baking stuff ready and waiting in your kitchen, yeah?"

Somewhere, we did. Somewhere under the masses of stuff my mum had brought home and behind the stacks of other people's memories blocking the kitchen doorway.

This was why it was safer to stay away from people. I cursed Mr Carroll in my head.

"Um, sorry. Can't. Mum's ... having some work done in the kitchen at the moment." I stumbled a little over the lie, but no one seemed to notice. "Plaster and loose tiles everywhere. We need somewhere else."

There weren't a whole lot of options, really. Slowly, we all turned to look at Grace, who stared back for a moment, then tutted.

"Fine. We'll do it at my place. My parents are out of town this weekend anyway." She looked at Ella. "But don't think I didn't notice that you didn't answer my questions."

Jasper wrapped an arm round Ella's shoulders protectively. "So, Saturday, ten o'clock at Grace's, then? Perfect. Who wants to go shopping for ingredients?"

I'd volunteered to buy the stuff for the mince pies so I knew we'd have exactly what we needed, when we needed it. With everything else that was going on, lying awake all Friday night wondering if Jasper would buy the right sort of mincemeat, or whether Yasmin would know that pastry needed cold butter, not room temperature, was more than I could deal with right now.

So on Friday after school I popped into the local supermarket, with my list and the money from Ella's gran for the ingredients. It was pretty busy, but I kept my head down and focused on what I needed. At least, until I heard a familiar voice across the aisle.

"There you are! I've been searching everywhere, Gran. You know you're not supposed to go out on your own." Ella sounded strained, tired.

I sneaked a glance up – I had a feeling this wasn't something she'd want me to see. Her blond hair was scraped back from her pale face and the shadows under her eyes were even darker than before.

Her gran, on the other hand, showed no signs of a lingering illness. Actually, she looked quite healthy. But very, very confused. Her eyes darted around her as if she wasn't sure where she was and she gripped the handle of her oversized carpet bag so tightly that her knuckles were white.

"Denise? Is that you?" she said, blinking up at her granddaughter.

Ella glanced round. I shrank back against the

shelves full of Christmas crackers and chocolate. "No, Gran, it's me. Ella. Aunt Denise is in Australia. Remember?"

"Ella. Of course." She shook her head. "I needed to get … something."

Slipping a hand through her gran's arm, Ella started to lead her towards the exit. "We've got everything we need at home, Gran. Remember? The man delivered it yesterday."

"Did he? Did he bring the biscuits?"

"He did," Ella said, her tone reassuring.

"Right." Gran looked up at her again. "So what do we need from here, then?"

Ella's steps faltered for a moment and, from behind, I could see her shoulders slump. "Nothing, Gran. It's time to go home."

As they made for the doors, I could hear Ella's gran still questioning. "Don't know why you brought me out in this weather, then. I'm an old lady, you know. Should be at home, keeping warm…"

The automatic doors swished closed behind them, but I kept staring. All the little lies that Ella had been telling began to slot into place. It looked like I wasn't the only one keeping secrets. And I didn't have any idea what to do about it.

MINCE PIES

1. Heat the oven to 200°C/fan 180°C/gas 6.

2. Rub 225g of cold, diced butter into 350g of plain
    flour, then mix in 100g of golden caster sugar and a
    pinch of salt.

3. Combine the pastry into a ball and knead it briefly.

4. Roll out the dough and cut out rounds to line a
    greased cupcake tin.

5. Spoon mincemeat into the cases and cut out smaller
    rounds to top the pies, pressing the edges gently
    together to seal.

6. Beat one small egg and use it to brush the top of
    the pies.

7. Bake for 20 minutes until golden.

8. Cool and dust with icing sugar.

Just walking up Grace's driveway on the Saturday morning made my shoulders tense up. The immaculate gardens, the beautifully trimmed box hedges leading up the empty drive to the huge blue front door, with its big brass knocker.

My house used to be this neat and tidy, even if it was only half the size. *God, imagine how much more Stuff Mum could fit in a house this big.*

"Are you coming, or what?" Jasper asked, and I felt grateful again that he'd suggested walking together. I wouldn't have wanted to arrive on my own.

"I'm coming." I hurried up the paved bricks to catch him before he knocked on the door. And when Grace answered, with barely a look at either of us, I followed him in without a pause.

I was a Bake Club member and this was a Bake Club event. I had every right to be here.

"Where's Mac?" Yasmin asked, as I put down my bag at the foot of one of Grace's shiny metal kitchen stools. The stainless steel counters were spotless, of course, as was the tiled floor, but what really caught my eye were the perfectly themed Christmas decorations. Lots of red and gold and sprouting greenery, and the occasional cherub, all looking utterly out of place in the ultra-modern kitchen.

"He said he might be a bit late," I said. "He'll be along eventually."

"I should hope so," Grace grumbled. "We need all the help we can get."

"More to the point, where's Ella?" I asked. "I need to double check her gran's recipe before we can start." I'd only written down the ingredients on my shopping list.

Jasper pulled his phone from his pocket. "Hang on. She texted me ... ten minutes ago. Says she's on her way. Something came up, apparently."

"Something with her gran?" I thought of the confused old woman being led out of the supermarket the night before. No wonder Ella was so worried all the time, not wanting people to know her gran couldn't bake her own cakes any more. And Ella's dad was still away, wasn't he? Was she looking after her gran all on her own?

"She didn't say," Jasper answered with a shrug, but I could see concern in the slight furrow between his brows. *Was this what they'd argued about at the party*, I wondered?

"Well, we can start getting the equipment and ingredients ready, anyway," I said, pulling my apron out from my bag. "Where are your mixing bowls and bun tins, Grace?"

She blinked at me blankly and I sighed. "OK. Let's start opening cupboards."

It took us a while – there were a *lot* of cupboards, mostly filled with pristine cooking equipment that looked barely touched – but eventually we had enough bowls, wooden spoons, and bun tins to be getting on with.

"How are we going to do this?" Yasmin asked, frowning at the top-of-the-range oven. "Massive as it is, I can't see us fitting a hundred plus mince pies in there all at once."

"We don't have the tins, anyway," I said. "I guess we'll need to do it in batches, the same way we did the biscuits on Thursday."

By the time Ella arrived, looking anxious, we were sorted. I wanted to talk to her, admit what I'd seen at the supermarket, but I knew she wouldn't relax enough to tell me the truth until the mince pies were done.

I was in charge of making the pastry, as I was the

only one who didn't pull a horrified face at the idea. I'd found an unused KitchenAid mixer still in its box at the back of one of the cupboards that I was itching to test out, so I wasn't too bothered.

Yasmin was in charge of rolling out and cutting the bottoms of the pies, Grace was adding the mincemeat – the only task she was willing to take on – and Jasper was doing the tops. We'd cook two trays at a time, making twenty-four pies. It would take us most of the day to get through seven lots, but we'd get there.

"Maybe we can use this on our application form too," Yasmin said, as she sorted through her cutters. "Like the Christmas cookies."

"No!" Ella said sharply, too loud, and Yasmin looked up in surprise, cutters clattering to the counter.

Ella looked down at her hands. "Um, Gran wouldn't want anyone to know she hadn't made them herself. She'd be ashamed."

"Right. So we won't use it, then," I said soothingly. I really needed to talk to Ella. There had to be something we could do to help her, something more than baking. But first, the mince pies. One thing at a time. "Are we ready to start?"

Ella blinked up at me, then looked at the mixer.

"Gran's notes say to rub the butter and flour together. It doesn't mention a mixer."

"Trust me, the mixer will be quicker," I said. "If I have to do seven batches of mince pies by hand, we'll be here until next Christmas."

"But will it taste the same?" Ella pressed. "They need to be perfect."

"It's exactly the same," I promised, trying not to sound impatient. They were going to be scoffed down in no time and no one would be able to tell the difference. "Trust me. You know me and perfect."

"Yeah," Ella said, clutching the recipe a little more tightly in her hand. "I know. It's just—"

"Oh, for God's sake," Grace snapped. "They'll be perfect, Ella. Little Miss OCD over here will make sure of that. What I want to know is why it matters so damn much."

We all looked at Ella. Apparently Grace hadn't got the "one thing at a time" memo. But now the question had been asked... I wanted to hear her answer.

"What's going on, Ella?" Jasper asked quietly. "You can trust us, you know."

"We want to help," Yasmin added.

Ella looked a little doubtfully at Grace.

"Even Grace." Yasmin gave Grace a stern look

133

that warned her not to argue.

Grace rolled her eyes. "Of course we do. I'm letting you use my house, aren't I?"

"You may as well tell us." I put my wooden spoon on the counter. "It doesn't look like we're going to start baking until you do. Besides," I gave her an apologetic look, "I saw you last night. At the supermarket."

Slumping down on to one of the stools, Ella said, "Then you already know." She rubbed her eyes with her fingertips. "OK. Fine. I'll tell you."

A bang on the door interrupted the moment and Grace scurried off to open it, returning seconds later with Mac. Even everything going on with Ella didn't stop my chest tightening at the sight of him. Out of school uniform, in battered jeans and a hoodie, he looked even hotter than usual.

"What's going on?" he asked, taking in the way we were all crowded round Ella.

"Ella's about to explain the real reason we need to bake a ridiculous number of mince pies today," Grace said. "Now shush."

Ella looked up at us. Jasper inched a little closer until he was practically touching her. "I told you my gran was ill, right?" Ella said, focusing on me.

Grace nodded. "You said it was a cold or

something."

"I lied."

"We figured," Jasper said. "So what is it really?"

"Her memory," Ella said, her gaze darting down to her hands. "It's not been great for ages, but this last couple of weeks... She keeps doing things like leaving the oven on and forgetting about it. She set fire to a tea towel the other day. I had to unplug the cooker and tell her it was broken."

"That's awful," I said. Something cold settled in my stomach at the thought of this girl, who looked like she might be knocked over by a strong wind, having to deal with a grandmother who was losing it. I should have known, long before I saw her in the supermarket. Should have asked. Should have guessed she was hiding something.

Just like me.

"Have you told your dad?" I asked.

Mac was frowning, his face full of concern. I caught his eye for a moment, and he gave me a tight half-smile.

Ella shook her head. "His business trip got extended. Every time I talk to him he sounds really stressed. He doesn't need this right now."

"Neither do you," Mac pointed out. He stood up straighter, looking older than sixteen all of a sudden.

"You're trying to hide the truth from everyone. You can't do that forever."

"I know," Ella said miserably. "But if I can just keep things going until Dad gets back, I know he'll sort it out."

Remembering what she'd told me the day we met, I frowned. "But your dad works away a lot, right? If your gran… If she doesn't get any better … what are you going to do? You can't just stay at home on your own while he's away."

Ella shook her head. "She'll get better. We'll figure something out. We have to. Because otherwise…"

"Otherwise what?" Jasper asked.

She turned to him, her eyes wide and sad. "My mum. She's been hinting that she'd like me to move up north with her for a while now, but I don't want to go. If Mum knew about Gran…"

"She'd make you move," Jasper finished for her. "Immediately, I bet."

"Yeah." Ella gave him an apologetic look. "I'm sorry I didn't tell you before. I just wanted everything to carry on as normal, until Dad got back."

Jasper didn't answer. His jaw clenched tightly, he looked like he was still thinking through all the implications of what we'd just learned. But with a hundred and fifty mince pies to make, we simply didn't have the time for that.

I picked up my wooden spoon. "Guess we'd better get baking, then."

It didn't take too long to whip up the first batch of dough in the mixer and pass it on to Yasmin to roll out. Beside me, Mac had grabbed another bowl and started mixing his own by hand, using his fingers to rub the butter into the flour.

"Having fun there?" I asked, reaching for the scales to start weighing out ingredients for the next batch.

"It feels better by hand," he said. "Like fixing a car."

I paused and watched him for a moment. He frowned with concentration and his fingers never stopped moving as they worked the butter into the flour. He'd taken off his hoodie now, and I could see the muscles moving under his long-sleeved T-shirt.

"You're really getting into this, aren't you?"

His fingers stopped. Shaking his hair out of his eyes, he looked up at me, suddenly nonchalant. "Hey, I'm just doing this for Ella."

"Sure you are. And the bread?"

He shrugged. "Maybe I'd like to leave secondary school with at least one useful skill."

"And baking bread could get you a job." Tilting

my head to the side, I watched him work again, imagining Mac behind a baker's counter, getting up at stupid o'clock to make the bread and the pastries. Amazingly, it wasn't all that hard to picture. He'd gone from knowing nothing at all that first week, to making pastry this week. He liked it.

"I don't need school to get a job," Mac said, staring into his bowl again. "I've got one waiting for me, full-time, the minute I get done with training."

"Your dad's garage." Was it me, or was he sounding less than enthusiastic about it? "That's what you want to do?"

His shoulders hunched. "It's what I'm good at. The only thing I know."

"So learn something new." I wasn't going to tell him that he should start studying, pass his GCSEs, do A levels, all that rubbish. That wasn't Mac.

But that didn't mean he only had one option, either. I knew what it felt like to be trapped, like there was no escape from the piles of Stuff waiting to crash down on you. But Mac was smart, he was talented, and he was stubborn. And I couldn't bear the thought of him stuck working with his dad and his brother for the rest of his life, if that wasn't what he wanted to do.

"What about a catering course?"

Mac glanced up at me and, maybe it was my imagination, but I swear I saw a spark of hope in his eyes. Before he could say anything, Ella bounded over, her gran's recipe still clutched in her hands, to see how we were getting on.

"Are we nearly there?" she asked, eyes wide with concern. "Only, it's getting late…"

"It's twelve o'clock, Ella," I said, as soothingly as I could. "We've got loads of time. Don't worry."

Mac tipped his dough out into the clingfilm and headed for the fridge. "And that lot makes three. Plus Lottie's is four. We're over halfway there."

"OK. Good." Ella's head bobbed nervously as she wandered off to check on Yasmin. I stared after her.

"You're worried about her," Mac said, and when I turned, I found him watching me.

"Aren't you?"

"She's not my problem," he said. But when I raised my eyebrows, he sighed. "OK, yeah. But I don't know how much we can do to help."

"Beyond making mince pies."

"Exactly."

Because of our factory-style set-up, Mac and I were finished before everyone else. But when I left the kitchen to try to figure out where the bathroom was in Grace's sprawling house, I noticed that Mac was taking over from Jasper in finishing off the pies.

If I'd been paying proper attention, I'd have realized that Ella had stopped nagging everyone – because she'd also left the room. All I thought was that this was further proof that Mac really did like baking. Not that, as I returned from a successful bathroom hunt, I was bound to stumble over Jasper and Ella having a very private moment under the mistletoe in the hallway.

"This is why you said no, isn't it?" Jasper said. "When I asked you out."

I ducked back behind the stairs to make sure they couldn't see me and considered my options. I couldn't slip past without them noticing, that much was clear. And if I made myself known now, it might be OK. They hadn't said much yet, after all. But then … if I interrupted them, they might never have this conversation. And it really looked like one that needed to be had.

Plus, I was nosy. So I stayed hidden by the stairs, edging forward to listen and watch. They wouldn't see me unless they turned and looked directly at me. But they were too wrapped up in each other.

"I said no because…" Ella tucked her pale hair

back behind her ears, like she was buying time before she spoke again. "It's not that I don't like you, Jasper, you know that."

"I should hope not." Jasper reached out and ran a finger down her face. "You seemed to like me when I kissed you at the party."

Ella's face flushed red. "I did. It's just ... with everything that's going on…"

"You need someone on your side. You need friends. You need me."

They stared at each other for a long moment, until Jasper glanced up and grinned. "Look. Mistletoe."

Ella stepped back. "I might have to move away. Really soon. And I don't know what's going to happen with Gran when my dad gets back. Or with my mum. And everything in my life is complicated. And—"

"And I don't care," Jasper said, still smiling. "I just want to kiss you."

He bent his head to hers and I looked away. Some things were too private even for me.

"That looks like fun." Mac's murmur by my ear made me jump. How had he got so close without me noticing? He was only centimetres away and I could smell the spices on his skin. "Think we can take the credit for getting them together?"

"How did you get there?" I whispered, the words harsh in the silence. Luckily, Ella and Jasper were far too preoccupied to notice.

Mac waved a hand behind him. "The other door from the kitchen. You did know there were two, right?"

I didn't. I could have escaped back to the kitchen at any time. "It's not like I've spent a lot of time here before."

"Yeah." Mac tilted his head to look at me, his blue eyes bright and so close I could almost count his eyelashes. "Why is that? Didn't you and Grace used to be, like, the stars of Drama Club? How come you weren't friends?"

I pulled a face, trying to lighten the moment. He was too close. It was playing havoc with my breathing. "I guess Grace doesn't like to share the limelight. Besides, like you ever paid any attention to what I did with my life after we left junior school, until you needed my help with the baking."

Mac tugged me closer, away from Jasper and Ella, deeper into the shadows of the stairwell, and my skin burned at the touch of his hands.

His gaze stayed fixed on my face the whole time, and I swallowed.

"That's not true," he murmured, his voice husky.

"I noticed things."

My eyes darted away for a moment, as if not looking at him meant he wasn't so very close. "Like what?" Because while everyone in the school noticed Mac, I knew I wasn't in the same league. Even before Dad died, I got on with my work, I did well in classes, I took part in the kind of activities that didn't involve any kind of sporting ability. Nothing special.

"In Year Seven," Mac said, a small smile on his lips, "we had to read that poem together in assembly. About leaves in autumn."

Heat flared in my cheeks. "That's what you remember? You know, I really don't mind if you forget that."

"In Year Eight," he went on, ignoring me, "you were Juliet when we were reading Shakespeare in English and you cried at the end."

"These aren't getting any better." But I couldn't stop looking at him, all the same. Mesmerized by his voice, my gaze held his as he spoke.

"In Year Nine, we went on that French exchange, and you got lost in that town we visited. The one with the stupid name. Mr Evans had to send out a search party."

"Not my fault..." I tried to explain, but Mac

wasn't listening.

"And in Year Ten, your dad died, and you stopped talking to anyone."

I looked away at last. "Yeah. Well..."

"Then this year, you got called to the Head of Year and said something that made him order me to join Bake Club."

My head jerked back up. He knew! "I didn't mean to. He just... He wanted..."

"I don't mind," Mac said, his voice still soft and low. "In fact, I'm kind of glad. I think I was on my last chance. If I hadn't taken this one, I'd probably be out of school by now. So whatever you said ... thank you."

The blue of his eyes was warmer than normal, somehow. And his mouth, that could twist up so mockingly when he wanted ... now it just looked soft and kind. I swallowed. "You're welcome." It hadn't been my intention. I'd been thinking much more about my own problems that day than about Mac's. But if he wanted to hold me responsible, I'd take that. Especially if he kept looking at me with that thoughtful expression.

The air around us changed again, as Mac's lips seemed to inch closer to mine.

"I can't believe you remember all those things

about me," I said, my words spilling out too fast. Why was I even talking? Why couldn't I just let something happen, rather than reason it away? "I think even I'd forgotten about the poem. I mean—"

"Lottie," Mac spoke my name firmly, but still quietly, and I shut up and looked at him again. "I remembered because…"

"Yeah?"

His eyes closed for a moment and he shook his head. When he opened them again, he gave me a rueful smile. "Because you're much more memorable than you think. That's why."

He stepped back and whatever tension there had been in the air disappeared. "Come on," he said. "Let's see how the assembly line is getting on."

I followed him into the kitchen, my mind still at the bottom of the stairs, thinking about what had just happened. I'd thought, for one lovely moment, that he was going to kiss me. Will Macintyre. Kissing me.

Until I'd ruined it.

Except … he *had* noticed me. He'd remembered me.

Because I was more memorable than I thought.

I couldn't help the grin that shot across my face. Mac thought I was memorable. And that made me a part of his life. And that was enough for me.

Back in the kitchen, the last batch of mince pies was in the oven, Ella was blushing in the corner and Jasper was dancing to some old Christmas song on the radio. I breathed in the spices and sugar in the air and it smelled like Christmas. As I made my way to the oven to check on the pies, Mac looked across at me from where he leaned against the windowsill and smiled.

Christmas was starting to look a little brighter.

CHRISTMAS MORNING MUFFINS

1. Heat the oven to 190°C/fan 170°C/gas 5.
2. Combine 225g of plain flour, 100g of caster sugar, 1 tsp of baking powder, 1 tsp of bicarbonate of soda and ½ tsp of salt together in a bowl.
3. Stir in 150g of fresh or dried cranberries.
4. Beat together 1 egg, 150ml of orange juice, 60ml of vegetable oil and 1 tsp of grated orange rind, then add to dry ingredients.
5. Stir until just combined, then divide equally between greased muffin cases in a 12-hole muffin tray.
6. Sprinkle tops lightly with caster sugar.
7. Bake for 15 to 20 minutes, until a cake tester or skewer comes out clean.

"So, Lottie, how are things today?" Mrs Tyler looked over her navy-framed glasses at me, as she did every week.

And as I did every week, I sat back in my chair and lied through my teeth.

"Everything's really good," I said, forcing some feeling into my voice. "Really. Mum and I are making plans for Christmas. Last year, it was so soon after everything happened, we didn't really bother. But this year we're coming up with new traditions to share together."

Mrs Tyler nodded enthusiastically. "Making new traditions? That sounds like a great idea. What have you come up with?"

"Um, well, the tree, for a start," I said, thinking of the three battered fake Christmas trees Mum had dragged home from the charity shop the week before. "We always used to have one huge tree in the hallway. But this year, we've got three smaller trees, one in the lounge, one in the kitchen and one upstairs in my room."

"That sounds nice," Mrs Tyler said.

"We're theme decorating them too," I added. "Mum's been reading a lot of home magazines lately." That much was true, anyway. She'd brought home a whole stack of them that the library were throwing out. I'd put the smallest of the fake trees on top of the stack. It looked pretty festive.

Well, as festive as our house was ever likely to look again.

"What else?" Mrs Tyler asked.

"Oh, well, Miss Anderson's teaching us to make her traditional Christmas Morning muffins this week in Bake Club." It never hurt to remind her that I was Taking Part In Things again. "I thought I could make them for Mum for Christmas breakfast this year."

"That sounds lovely. So you're enjoying Bake Club?"

"I really am," I said, trying not to sound too surprised at the fact. "I think I'd forgotten how much I love baking." And now I'd remembered, it had given me a new enthusiasm for, well, everything.

Maybe Dad had known just what he was doing when he taught me to bake.

"Have you thought about picking up any of your other old activities? I hear the Drama Club is still short of some fairies for *A Midsummer Night's Dream* next term."

I shook my head. "I think I'm going to keep focusing on school and Bake Club for now." Apart from anything else, I didn't fancy being a lowly drone fairy to Grace's Titania, Fairy Queen.

Mrs Tyler put down her pen and folded her hands over her pad of paper. My gaze wandered past her shoulder to the lonely string of red tinsel hanging from her book case and I was wondering whether Mum would have brought home any actual Christmas decorations when Mrs Tyler said, "I spoke to Miss Anderson yesterday."

My attention snapped back to her face again. "You did?"

Mrs Tyler nodded. "She said that you're a very valuable asset to Bake Club."

"That's ... good." The warm, proud feeling starting to grow in my chest was stifled by the way she said it. Like it couldn't be true. Or even as if it were a bad thing.

"She says you've grown very close to Will Macintyre."

So that was it. Of course. "I've been partnered

with him a few times," I said. "He's never really baked before, so he sort of needs the help."

"He doesn't have the best reputation at this school, does he?" Mrs Tyler said, obviously choosing her words carefully. But I knew what she meant. She didn't think he was an appropriate person for a grieving teen to be friends with.

Still, I shrugged and played innocent. "I think Mr Carroll was hoping that being part of Bake Club would help him settle down and get through the rest of the school year."

For all I knew, Mr Carroll had just run out of other ideas and didn't want to go through the paperwork of an expulsion. But I'd given Mrs Tyler something to think about. Probably she'd go and talk to Mr Carroll, but I'd bought myself a little time anyway, delaying the inevitable lecture on how to choose my friends.

"Perhaps," she said. "What about the other people in the group? Have you made many other friends?"

"Jasper's great," I said, without really thinking. "And Ella."

"Jasper. He's the one with the … hair."

"And the eyeliner," I added helpfully, mostly to watch her mouth purse in disapproval. But, fun as it was, I didn't really want her thinking I was going off the rails with the Goth kids and bad boys. She'd have me down on paper as depressed and rebellious in seconds, which would surely involve a phone call to Mum. "Ella's the year below us. Very sweet. Loves baking."

I could see Mrs Tyler trying to place Ella and her face cleared as she realized who I was talking about. "That's good. Girl friends are important in your teenage years."

How had this dinosaur got a job counselling children? She had to be giving all the other school counsellors a bad name. I wanted to point out that there was more to who you were friends with than their gender, or whether they wore eyeliner, or set fire to things. Well, maybe not that last one. Still...

But I stayed quiet. I pretended that Mac was a mere acquaintance, that Jasper was eccentric, that Ella was a sweet, uncomplicated girl with no problematic home life.

Ella's dad still wasn't back. This wasn't like my mum – this was far more serious. If I'd listened to all those high-school dramas on TV, I'd be talking to Mrs Tyler about Ella's gran, and getting her the help she needed.

But I didn't.

Because I needed Mrs Tyler to believe that I was happy, safe and trouble-free too.

I checked my watch; our time was nearly up. "I'd better get going," I said, with a false grin. "I hope you have a great Christmas." And that I never had to see her again. I was hoping that quite a lot. Surely a whole half term of these weekly meetings was enough to show her that I was fine?

"You too, Lottie." She flipped open her desk diary and my heart sank. "I'll see you on the second Thursday back. Usual time?"

"Of course," I said, feeling my smile slip.

"Enjoy your new traditions," she said.

I nodded and left, wondering if always being in a bad mood after sessions with Mrs Tyler counted as a tradition.

As I made my way across to Bake Club, the bitter December air biting through my jacket, I realized something. The problem with having found somewhere that felt like home, that had people in it that I liked and who liked me, was that I now had to spend two weeks – the two weeks most people spent with their nearest and dearest – away from them. Two weeks of just me and my mum and all the Stuff in our house. Who needed presents, when you could dig through a stack of empty, washed-out tins in search of the hidden surprises beyond?

Oh, look, a broken vase! And, now, what could this be? A mouldy magazine? You shouldn't have. No, really.

Maybe they'd want to get together and do something. Not at the school, of course. But maybe at someone's house... Except I couldn't suggest that, could I? Because even if anyone wanted to, if it was my suggestion, they'd assume I was inviting them round to my house.

Which was the one thing I could never, ever do.

So just me, Mum and the Stuff for Christmas. And Miss Anderson's Christmas Morning muffins.

The food technology classroom was already full by the time I got there. Mac looked up from our workstation and smiled at me, and the warm, close feeling from Grace's house was suddenly back. I smiled as best I could given my mood, but stopped by Ella and Jasper's station first.

"How did the Christmas Fair go?" I asked, leaning over the counter.

Jasper and Ella exchanged grins. "It was brilliant. Jasper helped me get everything over there, and Gran was having a better day, so we took her for a little bit too." Ella looked more relaxed than I'd ever seen her and Jasper was ruining his Goth look with another huge smile.

"I'm glad it worked out," I said, wishing my problems were so easily solved. Except Ella's weren't really, were they? Sure, the church had the mince pies they'd been promised, but there was still Ella's gran to deal with.

"And even better," Ella chattered on. "Dad's coming home tomorrow, in time for Christmas."

"He'll be able to fix things," Jasper said, with the assurance of someone who'd never been let down by a parent. Jasper's mum and dad might want to investigate every aspect of his existence, but he always had their attention and their willingness to help.

He didn't know how lucky he was.

I tried to look happy for them. "That's great, Ella. I'd better…" I motioned towards Mac and they nodded.

"Everything OK over there?" Mac asked, as I got closer.

"Apparently so. The season of miracles has worked its magic again." I sounded bitter, I knew, but he wouldn't call me on it.

"Miracles? I seem to remember mixing a lot of pastry dough and it didn't feel that miraculous at the time." But then he looked at me and from the way his eyes darkened, I knew he was thinking about what else had happened that day.

155

I swallowed and tried to find something to say. Something light. "A hundred and fifty mince pies in a day? That sounds pretty amazing to me."

"Well, maybe we're all magicians, then. We made it happen."

He was right. We'd changed Ella's Christmas for the better. I didn't know which felt best – helping out a friend or just realizing that I could make a difference. I could change things. And if I could change this, maybe I could change my own life too. And Mum's.

"We did." I looked up at him, and the tight feeling in my chest contracted just a little bit more.

But then Miss Anderson walked in, clapping her hands, and Mac looked away.

"Great! You're all here," Miss Anderson said. "I wanted to tell you… I've mailed our application for the competition! And I've been thinking about some other things we could do, as a club. How would you feel about a day's work experience in one of the local bakeries?"

That actually sounded fun. As much as I really, really wanted to do well in the competition, maybe I should be thinking about the world after school too. About a career, even. Getting real experience would be more useful than winning a competition, wouldn't it?

"It would be a good opportunity for you all to see how a real bakery is run. Just in case any of you are considering baking as a career choice."

Beside me, Mac stiffened and, when I looked up, he was scowling. Was he thinking about it too? Or was he just thinking about how his dad would react if he did?

"So what do you think?" Miss Anderson looked round the class expectantly.

Yasmin and Grace were in enthusiastic agreement.

"It's a great idea, miss," Yasmin said.

Grace nodded. "It could be a really interesting opportunity."

Jasper and Ella seemed less excited, but they both agreed.

"Don't bakers get up really early, though?" Jasper asked, frowning.

Miss Anderson ignored him and turned to our workstation. Mac was still glowering out of the nearest window, so I answered for both of us. "Sounds great."

She let out a little whoop. "Well, OK, then. I'll talk to some people, see what I can set up. But back to today – I just can't wait to share these muffins with you. So if you'll all get your ingredients out..."

Her cranberry-orange muffins were a nice, easy

fix for the last session of term, and they smelled delicious — a spicy, Christmassy scent, mixed with the sharp, tangy smell of the fruits. Mac and I baked mostly in silence, his weird bad mood hovering over us like a cloud.

While the muffins cooked, we all set about clearing up, as normal, until Miss Anderson stopped by our station.

"I wanted to talk to you both," she said.

I draped my tea towel over the cabinet handle to dry and turned to listen. Mac, however, kept on washing up. "This work experience could be a really big opportunity for you. A chance to see what options there are out there after school. You both have real talent in the kitchen, and I'd love to help you take that further. So I'd like you both, more than anyone, to try and get some practice in over the holidays. I'm going to be coming up with all sorts of challenges and projects to get you ready for the competition next term and I want you at the top of your game."

My heart was sinking, but I managed a tight smile for her. "Of course."

"Great!" Miss Anderson beamed. "You two keep your eyes on the prize. It could be the start of great things for you!"

A splash behind me made me turn, just in time

to see Mac stalking out of the classroom, drying his hands on his trousers as he went. I bit my lip, and looked up at Miss Anderson's disappointed face.

"I'll talk to him," I said, and followed Mac out into the corridor, ignoring the fascinated looks of the others as I walked past.

It wasn't hard to find him. I just followed the sounds of crashing and swearing.

"What did that poor, innocent wall ever do to you?" I asked, leaning against a display on food hygiene to watch him slap his palm against the wall again.

"What do you care?" he asked, turning and pacing away from me.

"I told Miss Anderson I'd talk to you." I didn't want to admit my own reasons for checking up on him.

"Like she cares."

Which was ridiculous. Why would she have bothered to talk to us about the work experience if she didn't care?

"She wants to help," I tried. "She doesn't know about … your situation." Or mine, I wanted to add. It was hard to muster the necessary sympathy for Mac when he didn't even realize I was in exactly the same boat.

Mac spun towards me, colour high in his cheeks

159

and his hair a mess. He looked wild. Out of control.

"Exactly!" he said, throwing up his arms as he stepped closer. "She doesn't know. Of course I'd love to take up these chances, see where they lead. Yeah, maybe I want to break out. To get away from Dad and the garage and the rest of my stupid, bloody future. Maybe I want to do something new, something I love. And maybe that could be baking. But how can I?"

"Look, I know things are difficult with your dad—" I started.

"What do you know?" That mouth, the one that had looked so soft, so inviting, under the stairs at Grace's house, curled up into a sneer. "You, with your perfect house, your perfect kitchen, where you can cook your perfect muffins any time you like. What the hell do you know about any of it?"

I wanted to tell him. The bitterness rose up inside me, like a burning acid in my throat. He was practically shouting in my face and I wanted nothing more than to yell back. To scream and shout and tell him everything. About Mum and the Stuff, Mr Carroll and Mrs Tyler, and how if he thought it was hard practising baking when his dad wasn't looking, he should try doing it when you couldn't even clear a path to the oven. When you had no dad to get mad at you.

I wanted to rage at him and hurt him with the truth. But I couldn't. So I did something even worse.

I kissed him.

Grabbing his arms, I rose up on tiptoes and pressed my mouth against his, more to make him stop talking and to stop myself from blurting out the truth than anything else.

For the first moment, it felt angry, but then … my grip loosened on Mac's arms, just as I felt his hands come up to rest against my back, holding me to him. The kiss grew softer, more real, and I melted against him, wanting more.

And he wanted it too. I didn't know what this was between us, but there was no mistaking the way his fingers traced up to my neck, or the noise he made, right at the back of his throat, as he pulled me closer.

"Oh!" The surprised sound from behind Mac made me jump back. Mrs Tyler stood by the door at the other end of the corridor, her eyes wide. "Lottie! I think we should—"

I didn't wait to find out what she thought. Jerking out of Mac's arms, I turned and dashed back to the food tech classroom, not even looking back to see if either of them followed me.

Mrs Tyler. Of all the people it could have been, why did it have to be her?

Everyone stared at me as I marched back into Bake Club, my heart still racing. Could they tell what I'd been doing? Or were they just worried about Mac? They stared just as hard at him when he followed me in, a few minutes later.

But he didn't look at me at all.

I was halfway out of the school gates when I heard Mac calling after me. I'd said my goodbyes to everyone in class, lingering a moment after they left, trying to think of the best way to ask Miss Anderson for extra baking time and failing. It would have to wait until after the school holidays. I'd hoped everyone else – especially Mrs Tyler – had disappeared, but apparently not.

I paused by the gates and waited for him to catch up with me.

"I thought you'd gone home," I said as he reached me. Was it just the cold making my lungs feel tight? Or was it the way his hair fell almost into those too-blue eyes? The way he looked at me, maybe, like he couldn't see anything else in the world right now.

"I was waiting for you."

I swallowed. "Why?"

"I wanted to apologize." He gave me a lopsided smile. "I shouldn't have taken it out on you. It's not your fault I can't bake at home."

"Yeah, well. I'm sorry I kissed you." I'm sorry I kissed you? What kind of idiot says that? He was too close to me, that's what it was. It messed with my brain.

"You never have to apologize for that." Cold fingers brushed against my cheek as he tucked my hair behind my ear. "Although the running-away part was a bit of a let-down."

I could feel the heat of a blush on my cheeks. "Sorry. It was just … Mrs Tyler…"

"I get it. I'm not the kind of guy you want the school counsellor to see you with."

I wanted to deny it, but how could I? "Sorry."

Mac glanced away, just for a moment. "I'm used to it. And I had another reason for wanting to catch you before you left."

"Yeah?"

"I wanted to wish you a Merry Christmas. Properly."

"Oh yeah. Um, me too. Hope you have a good one."

His smile was soft as he lifted a hand to my face again. Slowly, he lowered his mouth to mine – so slow that this time I had a chance to register every heartbeat. The way his eyes fluttered shut, even as I kept staring at his eyelashes. Our breath, misting together in the freezing air. How his hand slipped down to my shoulder, then to the back of my neck, holding me close.

His lips met mine and my eyes closed of their own accord, sinking into the kiss. It wasn't long, barely more than a few seconds. But it blew me away more than the angry kiss we'd shared in the corridor.

Mac pulled back, just a little. "Merry Christmas, Lottie," he murmured, against my lips.

I swallowed. "Merry Christmas."

His hand slid away from my neck, back to his side. Somewhere across the road, a horn beeped and Mac's head jerked up. "That's Jamie. I gotta go." He gave me a small smile. "See you."

I nodded, too stunned to ask when, too astonished to even follow him with my eyes as he jogged away towards his brother's car. Instead, I leaned back against the frosty brick pillar holding the school gates, and reran what had just happened.

Until I looked up and saw Mrs Tyler frowning at me across the car park.

Hell. Looked like next term would be even more interesting than I'd thought.

ASPARAGUS QUICHE

1. Heat the oven to 190°C/fan 170°C/gas 5.
2. Roll out 225g of shortcrust pastry thinly and use to line a 20-cm flan ring.
3. Bake blind for 25 minutes.
4. Melt 25g of butter in a pan and stir in 25g of flour to form a roux. Cook over a gentle heat, stirring continuously for 2 minutes, then remove from heat.
5. Mix 150ml of milk with 150ml of liquid from a 425g tin of asparagus spears and season to taste.
6. Add the liquid gradually to the roux, stirring all the time, until the sauce thickens over a gentle heat.
7. Cool slightly and pour into flan ring.
8. Sprinkle 25g of cheddar cheese over and arrange the asparagus spears to form the spokes of a wheel then sprinkle another 25g of cheese on top.
9. Turn the oven up to 200°C/fan 180°C/gas 6.
10. Return to oven and cook for 5 to 10 minutes, until the cheese has melted.

Christmas sucked.

Last year, our first Christmas without Dad, had been beyond awful and we'd mostly just ignored the holiday altogether. This year, when things were *supposed* to be getting back to normal, Christmas just sucked.

All the things that used to make it, well, Christmassy, were missing. No magazine-perfect tree with coordinating wrapped presents underneath. None of Dad's mince pies and no sip of sloe gin as a treat on Christmas Eve. No family nearby to visit. No Boxing Day party for all of Mum and Dad's friends, just a card or two from the ones who still tried, saying they'd like to see us sometime. Mum hid them under a pile of magazines. No outings, no pantomime, no friends stopping by with gifts. Nothing.

Instead, Mum hummed Christmas carols as she turned magazines into paper chains to string from our ceilings – the only previously unoccupied space in the house – all the while giving me a smug look, as if to say, *See? I told you they'd come in useful for something.*

Because, obviously, what we really needed was more clutter that I knew would stay up long past Twelfth Night. Loads more useful than, say, a skip to get rid of all the Stuff.

But it wasn't really all Mum's fault. Actually, it was nice to see her putting in a bit of an effort. Yes, Christmas dinner was two microwaved mini roast dinners, and yes, my presents were mostly Stuff wrapped in charity-shop paper. But we did watch a couple of Christmas films, while eating shop-bought mince pies – Mum collecting up the tinfoil cases and wiping them out, in case she needed them later. And for the odd moment, it felt a little bit like we were a family again, even if there were only two of us now.

No, the thing that sucked the most about Christmas, after missing my dad, wasn't Mum. It was Mac.

We hadn't made plans. I was too blindsided by his kiss to even think of asking for his phone number. But it's not like he couldn't have found me, if he'd wanted to. I kept a close eye on my phone throughout the holidays, checking in on the usual websites, updating my status to see if he commented ... but he never did.

Jasper and Ella, on the other hand, were constantly in touch.

"Has he called yet?" Jasper asked, excitement vibrating over the computer screen. The joy of Skype. I could see the two of them huddled close on a sofa, in the middle of a spotless lounge, beaming identical happy smiles at me, while I hid in my room so they couldn't see the Stuff.

I sat on my bed, laptop on my knee. "No. Not in the eight hours since we last spoke."

Ella's smile drooped a little. "I thought maybe he'd call late at night. You know, for a secret moonlit chat. Brooding romantic style. He seems the sort."

"No, he doesn't," I said. "And remind me, which one of us did he kiss and then not contact for two weeks? Because you're the ones who keep bringing it up." I grinned, so they knew I was joking.

Jasper rolled his eyes. "Ella's excited about us going on dates together or something."

I couldn't really see Mac as the double-dating sort. Or, on current evidence, dating me at all. "What's your excuse, then?"

"I like to make her happy," Jasper said and Ella made a soppy noise and rested her head on his shoulder. But I knew that wasn't all, so I waited. "Fine, fine. I don't know. You seem ... brighter when you're with him. Happier. I like you happy too. Is that so bad?"

"No." Actually, it was nice to have friends to care about me. I'd missed that, even if I hadn't realized it at the time.

"Besides, the suspense is killing me," Jasper added, making Ella laugh.

"You and me both." I sighed. "Well, I'll see him back at school tomorrow, one way or another." Of course, I'd probably also see Mr Carroll and Mrs Tyler. After last term, I had no doubt they'd be watching me even more closely than normal. Hard to have a meaningful talk with Mac when I had to keep checking to see if they were watching.

And by "meaningful chat" I obviously meant another kiss.

"I still say we should have gone and walked past his dad's garage. Just casually. On our way to somewhere else," Ella said. This was a plan of action she'd been suggesting since the first day of the Christmas holidays, when they called to find out what was going on with Mac storming out of Bake Club and I cracked and confessed under their intense questioning.

"Because that wouldn't be in any way suspicious," I replied. Of course, I hadn't told them that I'd walked past the garage three times since the start of the holidays and not even managed a glimpse of Mac.

"You could just call him, of course," Jasper pointed out.

"I don't have his number."

"I could give it to you."

"No, thanks."

"You're hopeless."

"I'm fine," I countered. "Now, more importantly, what's going on with you guys? What did your dad say about your gran, Ella?"

"He's going to talk to his boss. See if he can work out of the local office full-time, instead of all the travelling." Ella still sounded a little nervous about it all, but Jasper burst in with more excitement.

"If he's at home, her mum will have no reason to make her move!"

"I hope it works out," I said. A subtle reminder to Jasper that things didn't always go to plan, and it might not be a good idea to get Ella's hopes up.

Apparently it was a little too subtle. "Of course it will! Anyway, we've got to go. I've got our day all planned out."

Ella perked up at that. "See you tomorrow!"

"Yeah. You two have fun."

"We will!" Skype clicked off and I pushed the

computer off my lap on to the bed.

The last day of the holidays. There was a time when this would have been a day spent trying to enjoy every last moment of my freedom before I had to go back to school. Dad always used to take the last day of the holidays off work and we'd go out somewhere, anywhere, just to make the most of the day.

This holiday, I wasn't even sure it was worth leaving my room. At least here, in my space, I could see the floor and the surfaces. It seemed as soon as Mum started holding on to Stuff, I'd started to let go.

I liked it. The space felt calming.

In the end, I spent the day getting things ready for school – finishing up last checks of homework, reorganizing my pencil case, making sure my uniform was clean and ironed. Mum stuck her head out of her door briefly that afternoon to see if there was anything I needed.

"You got me those five hundred biros at the pound shop in October," I reminded her. "I think I'm covered."

"That was a great deal," she said, and disappeared back into her room.

And that night, I curled up in bed with an old baking book of Dad's, rescued from a stack of Stuff, and imagined all the things I might bake with Mac that term.

School started back on a Thursday, which always felt weird, but at least meant I had Bake Club that afternoon. Even better, Mrs Tyler was away on some training day, so I had a reprieve from counselling until the following Thursday. I was not looking forward to hearing her thoughts on the inappropriateness of Mac.

"I want you to up your game this week," Miss Anderson said, as we all gathered round her in the food tech classroom. All, that is, except for Mac, who was nowhere to be seen. I tried to pay attention to what Miss Anderson was saying, but to be honest, most of my attention was on the door.

"The competition is just after half-term, and we've got a lot of work to do before then. So I hope you've all been practising over Christmas." She beamed, as what she obviously thought was a fantastic idea came to her. "Why don't we go round the class, before we start, and talk about what we baked over the Christmas holidays?"

Worst idea ever. Even more so because, just as she spoke, the door opened and Mac walked in. "And we can start with Mac," Miss Anderson said, beaming at him.

Mac stalled in the doorway. He looked taller. Broader than I remembered. I bet he'd been working in the garage all through the holidays. I bit my lip, unable to look away. Nerves fought excitement in my chest. This was what I'd waited for, all holiday. A chance to see him, talk to him. To find out what was going to happen next between us.

"Start what with me?" he asked, shaking raindrops from his hair as he dumped his bag on the side and took off his coat.

"We're talking about what we all baked this holiday," Grace filled in, batting her eyelashes at him. "So? What about you?"

Mac glanced over at me and I saw a flash in his eyes before his face shut down. Anger and frustration. And somehow, his frustration with his situation had found its focus in me. Because he thought I had a charmed and perfect life and I couldn't tell him how wrong he was.

The excitement faded away and I looked down at my hands. No wonder he hadn't called, if that was what he remembered every time he looked at me.

"Uh, well, mince pies, I guess," Mac said, making his way across the classroom to our workstation as he spoke. Was he talking about that day at Grace's? That wasn't quite the holidays, but I supposed it was close enough. Clever. "I liked making the pastry."

"Great!" Miss Anderson turned to me. "What about you, Lottie?"

I froze. What should I say? If I lied and talked about all the imaginary delicacies I'd created, Mac would just get more annoyed. But if I was honest and told them I hadn't touched anything more than a microwave and a toaster since school broke up, everyone else would be mad at me for not working hard enough for the club. I couldn't win.

In the end, I thought back to the old recipe books I'd been flicking through the night before and spun a picture of my perfect life again. Keeping my home life secret mattered more than Mac feeling bad about his own life. I had to remember that.

"Um, well, I made a crumble for Christmas Eve dinner, and some more mince pies for Christmas Day. And your muffins, for Christmas breakfast." Just like I'd told Mrs Tyler I would. Actually, I'd frozen the ones we had made in class in the tiny ice box above our fridge, then defrosted them in the microwave, but I was pretty sure that wasn't going to cut it for the competition.

"Lovely!" Miss Anderson looked touched that I'd taken on her family tradition. I felt a hot shame flooding over me when I thought how disappointed she'd be if she ever learned the truth.

Which was why, of course, I had to make sure no one ever did.

As she went round the rest of the room, I tuned out the list of culinary specialities my friends had helped to create, or learned to make, over the holidays. Instead, I turned to Mac, leaning into him just a little, just enough to let him know I was there. "How was your Christmas?" I murmured.

He turned his head just enough that I could see his mouth, his eyes. For a moment, the resentment in them lingered. Then he shook his head, just a little, and smiled at me, making the muscles in my shoulders relax at last. "The usual. Yours?"

Maybe there was hope for us after all.

"Boring."

"Yeah…" His gaze darted away. "Look, I… Well, I was going to call, but … things were really busy at the garage and Dad had lots he needed me to do."

"Sure." Except he'd never been there when I walked past. Maybe he was in the back, though. What did I know?

"But I was thinking—" he started, but cut himself off as Miss Anderson clapped her hands together.

We both straightened up to listen as she said,

"Well, today we're going to be building on all that practice you've been getting over the holidays. So far, most of what we've baked has been sweet, but the regional heats have a pairs challenge round, as well as the individual and group ones. We won't know until the day what you have to bake for that. And it could be savoury, which is why we're starting this term with a shortcrust pastry for a quiche. Now this might look simple enough, but there are important skills to learn here. Including baking blind. Which, before you ask, does not include cooking with your eyes closed. So…"

It seemed that Miss Anderson was taking this competition really seriously, so it looked like whatever Mac had been thinking was going to have to wait.

Eventually, we got out our bowls and ingredients and started baking, but even then Miss Anderson was much more attentive than usual, hovering over our workstations and offering advice. In one lull when she was over with Jasper and Ella, I asked Mac, "So … what were you thinking?"

He shook his head. "Doesn't matter now. But maybe … maybe we should, I don't know. Talk?"

Talk. I let out a long breath of relief. Boys were notoriously rubbish at talking about things that mattered and I'd kind of expected Mac to be worse than most. For once, I was happy to be proved wrong. "Yeah. Yeah, that would be good."

I had so many things I wanted to ask him. Starting with why he'd kissed me again, after the kiss in the corridor, and what it meant. Were we together now? Or was it just a spur-of-the-moment thing? And, most importantly, when was he planning on doing it again?

"After Bake Club?" Mac twirled the handle of his wooden spoon between his fingers. "We could, maybe, go for a coffee? Or something?"

That, right there, sounded almost like a date.

"I'd love to."

Even Mac looked a little relieved to have that much sorted and we both turned our attention back to our pastry, just in time for Miss Anderson's latest visit.

"That's looking really good, Mac," she said, peering into his bowl. "Obviously all that practice with the mince pie pastry was worth it!"

He didn't even look up at her as she spoke, and when she glanced over at me, all I could manage was a tight smile. She wandered off again, brow furrowed.

"You could tell her," I tried, but Mac cut me off.

"That's not happening."

"She might be able to get us some extra time

to practise here," I pointed out. And, actually, that would be perfect. I felt a little bad about using Mac's problems to solve my own, but really, if it meant we both got to do the necessary baking practice, did it matter how it happened?

Mac made a dismissive noise somewhere at the back of his throat and threw his wooden spoon down on to the counter before dumping out his pastry, ready to roll it. "More likely she'd want to talk to my dad about my future, try and convince him. She's that sort. The sort of teacher who thinks people just don't understand why she's right yet, and they just need her to explain it to them." He shook his head. "And trust me, that won't work with my dad."

"OK," I said, disappointment heavy in my stomach. "Guess you know him best."

"I do. And I don't need anybody's help dealing with him." Which put a pretty definite end to that idea.

But that still left us with the original problem. We both needed somewhere to practise if we wanted any chance of doing well in the competition and neither of us could do it at home. So far, the only place we'd managed to bake outside school was ... Grace's house.

I didn't want to ask; didn't want to have to owe

her, or beg her. But if it meant Mac and I got to practise our baking … it was worth it.

I waited until we'd finished clearing up and Mac was distracted by some of Jasper's endless questions, then slipped across the room to Grace and Yasmin's station.

"Come to check on the competition?" Grace asked, delicate blond eyebrows raised.

I bit back a retort. Instead, I said, "I'm thinking more about the group competition, actually."

"Really?" Yasmin looked interested at this. "What are you thinking we should bake?"

"I hadn't got that far, actually," I admitted. "I was just thinking that maybe it would do us all good to practise together."

"Why?" Grace cast her gaze round the classroom. "We already all bake here once a week. Isn't that enough?"

"But we don't, not really," I pointed out. "We bake in pairs, like we will for the challenge round. The only time we've ever baked things all together was when we did the Christmas biscuits with the Year Sevens, and the mince pies we made—"

"At my house," Grace finished for me. "So that's what this is about. You want to start holding baking parties at my house."

"Well, it is the biggest," Yasmin agreed. "And it would be good to get that practice in."

But Grace still looked suspicious. "I don't see why it has to be at my house. Why can't we use your perfect kitchen for a change?"

Well, that obviously wasn't an option. But both Grace and Yasmin looked at me, waiting for an answer.

I rubbed my hands against my school skirt. "Look, the thing is ... it's Mac."

I swear I could almost see Grace's ears perk up at the mention of his name. "Mac? What about him?"

I hated this. Hated using Mac's problems as a way to get what I wanted. But it was the only way to fix things for *both* of us.

"He can't bake at home – his dad would have a fit if he knew he was still coming here every week. He's a great baker. But if we want him on form for the competition, he needs to practise."

Yasmin looked sympathetic, but Grace's eyes narrowed. "Then why aren't you just dragging him home to your kitchen? Since you two seem so *close* these days."

Was that what she was mad about? Grace had never made a secret of the fact she fancied Mac. I wondered if Jasper had been talking. I couldn't imagine Mac would have told Grace about our kiss, and I certainly hadn't.

But Grace always wanted to be the star attraction, and if she thought I'd got the attention of the hottest guy in school… Well, I still remembered how she reacted after I got the junior lead in Drama Club. I didn't imagine she'd take this any better.

"Mac, he, well…" I tried to find the right way to put it. "He doesn't want anyone to know. About his dad. So don't mention it, OK? He certainly wouldn't like it if he thought I was taking pity on him. But if it's all of us, baking together, that might be OK. And it might get a bit cramped with six of us trying to bake in my kitchen." Especially since you couldn't currently clear a path to the oven.

"Fine," Grace said eventually. "Saturday mornings, then. My house. You're in charge of recipes and ingredients."

"Works for me," I said, feeling the tightness in my chest loosen. "I'll figure out how much everyone needs to chip in and let the others know."

"Let the others know what?" Mac asked from behind me, and I turned to grin at him.

"We're all going to practise baking on Saturday mornings at Grace's house," I said. "Ready for the competition."

Mac raised his eyebrows at Grace, who smiled very sweetly at him. "Lottie told us about your little problem with your dad," she said, and I felt Mac go very still beside me.

Damn her! I should have known she'd use this to try and get between me and Mac, especially as I told her not to. But what choice did I have?

"Of course I was happy to help, any way I can." She reached out to place a hand on his arm, a sign that when he got bored of me, she'd still be there, prettier, blonder and waiting.

But Mac jerked away, out of reach. "Lottie," he said, then stalked off towards our workstation, obviously expecting me to follow.

"I'm not a dog, you know," I said, catching him up. "I don't heel when you say my name."

"Sorry," he said reflexively, then scowled. "Wait. You told them about my dad when I asked you not to. You should be apologizing, not me." He glared down at me.

"Look, I'm sorry. But I had to!" Surely he understood that. "We needed somewhere to practise, all of us together. You most of all."

"I manage fine," Mac said.

"For now, sure. But it's going to get harder, and we need to practise a lot, if we want to do well in this competition." His expression didn't soften. "This could be your way out, but we need to get better. I was *helping* you." And myself, but I couldn't tell him that. Couldn't tell him I'd been lying to him, all along. What if he decided to tell my secret, like I'd told his?

"So, what? You're waiting for a thank you?" Mac shook his head, gripping the edge of the counter, like he was trying to stop himself banging his fist on it. "It wasn't your secret to tell."

Then he grabbed his coat and his bag and walked out, leaving his quiche still sitting on the counter. And leaving me staring helplessly after him, knowing that everyone else was watching.

God, how had I screwed up something so good, so quickly?

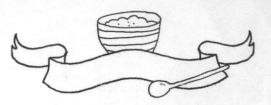

GRANDMA'S GINGERBREAD

1. Heat the oven to 160°C/fan 140°C/gas 3.

2. Melt 150g of golden syrup with 100g of butter and 150ml of milk in a pan.

3. Add an egg and mix in, allowing it to cook a little.

4. Beat in 200g of sieved flour, 3 tsp of ground ginger and 1 tsp of bicarbonate of soda.

5. Pour into a prepared 900g loaf tin and bake for 45 minutes, before turning down to 150°C/fan 130°C/gas 2 for the last 20 minutes.

Mac avoided me the whole next week. No talk about the kiss or about us. No talk at all. Ella looked sad whenever she saw me, and even Jasper had started giving me sympathetic glances after Mac didn't show up to the Saturday morning baking practice at Grace's house.

By the following Thursday, I'd gone past defensive into upset, straight through frustrated and now I was downright angry. Fine, maybe I shouldn't have said anything. Maybe it wasn't my secret, but I was trying to help him! Well, help both of us.

But whether I was wrong or not, ignoring me didn't help anyone. And after two weeks of not being able to talk about things over Christmas, especially that incredible kiss, I had every intention of cornering Mac until he told me what the hell it meant. Even if he never spoke to me again afterwards. At least I'd know.

First I had to get through another endlessly boring session with Mrs Tyler.

"So, Lottie." She pushed her glasses up her nose and stared at me. "I think there are a few things we need to talk about this week."

I slumped back in my chair. "Like?"

"William Macintyre." She tilted her head to the side. I assumed she'd seen someone do it on TV when they were acting sympathetic, because it didn't look at all natural on her.

"I know that youth culture today is all about the 'bad boy'." She actually made the air quotes. I barely resisted the urge to roll my eyes. "But, Lottie, as a grown woman, I can tell you that's not what you should be looking for in a life partner. Someone like Mac won't give you long-term happiness. And that's what you need to be thinking about."

"I've not even taken my GCSEs," I pointed out. "I'm not sure I need to be thinking about forever just yet." Besides which, we'd kissed twice – both hideously witnessed by the dinosaur on the other side of the desk – and he wasn't currently speaking to me. I really didn't think I needed to be worrying about our future.

Mrs Tyler sighed. "I've seen this story far too often, Lottie. Good girl falls for bad boy, goes off the rails, ruins her chances in life. Sometimes the girls get out soon enough to get back on the straight and narrow. Sometimes they … don't."

Way to make me a cliché. And to assume that every teenage girl was the same, destined to be led astray by good-looking boys. It would be easy enough to get out of the conversation, to tell her we weren't speaking and that there was nothing to worry about. But I didn't.

"Mrs Tyler, have my grades slipped this last term?"

Eyebrows jumping up in surprise, she glanced down at my file, open on the desk. "No. Actually, they're up on last year."

"What about Mac's?" I sat back and waited while she pulled out his file, half hidden under a stack of other papers on her desk.

"Also up," she said, not sounding particularly happy about it. "He did better than expected in his mocks last term." She glanced up at me. "Not that I should be telling you that. The results aren't official yet."

"So wouldn't you say it's just possible that instead of him pulling me down, being in Bake Club and being friends is boosting us both up?" I tried not to sound gloating, but it's pretty hard when you're *that* right.

Mrs Tyler just sighed again. "You think you can change him."

"I don't think he needs changing." Apart from the not-talking-to-me part. "He's my friend and I think he's a great person. And I think Bake Club is giving him the chance to show that to other people."

The bell rang. Time up.

I grabbed my bag and flashed Mrs Tyler an insincere smile. "See you next week."

And then I headed for the food tech classroom, ready to yell at Mac for being an idiot.

Continuing Miss Anderson's plan to "stretch us as bakers", we'd been asked to try out our own recipes for the first time. "Find a family recipe if you can," she'd suggested. "Something with meaning behind it, or memories. Something you can make your own speciality."

I'd brought ingredients for my dad's famous Dutch apple pie, but as I walked to the class, I wondered if I'd got enough for two. After all, what kind of family recipes was Mac likely to have? From the little I knew, his mum hadn't been around since he was tiny and it didn't seem likely that his dad ever whipped up fairy cakes at the weekend. Maybe we could make two smaller pies. That would be something to get us talking again. He'd see I was only trying to help him, at least. That I cared.

But all thoughts of Mac flew from my brain the moment I walked into the classroom.

"Jasper?" Gone was his constant after-school companion, the black hoodie. His eyes were liner-free, and his hair... "You're ... blond?"

"Light golden brown," Ella said, from beside him. She wasn't smiling. "The woman who sold us the hair dye said it was more transitional."

"Obviously," I said, still baffled. "But, um ... why?"

Jasper straightened his already perfectly vertical school tie. "Ella's mum is in town. We're going out to dinner tonight."

"So this is you making a good impression?" That made a kind of sense. But it seemed a shame that after pretending to be so many things to confuse his mum and dad, Jasper was now acting as someone else to please parents that didn't even belong to him.

"This is him being *normal*," Ella said, somehow making normal sound like an infectious disease.

"I'm trying to be a good influence," Jasper corrected her. "I want your mum to think you have a nice group of friends here."

"Dad's boss is dragging his feet on the local office contract thing. So Mum is talking about me moving up north with her," Ella explained. "Jasper's hoping we can convince her that if she takes me away from all the nice friends I have here, I'm bound to fall in with a bad crowd at my new school and ruin my life."

"Then don't tell her about Mac," I said, without thinking. At, of course, the exact moment he walked into the classroom.

Luckily, since he was still avoiding me, he headed straight for our workstation at the back of the class, showing no sign that he'd heard me at all. My heart sank. "I'd better..." I waved a hand towards where Mac had dumped his bag on the counter.

Jasper gave me a sympathetic smile. "Good luck."

"Thanks." I had a feeling I was going to need it.

Mac had a stack of ingredients strewn across the counter by the time I reached him. There was no order to them and no real way to guess what he was making. But I got the feeling that the higgledy-piggledy distribution was purely to irritate me.

"What are you making?" I asked, leaning against the cluttered counter.

"My grandma's gingerbread." He didn't look at me as he replied, his gaze still fixed on a crumpled piece of paper which I guessed held the recipe.

"That sounds good." Biting my lip, I decided to push my luck. "Want any help?"

"I think I can manage." He gave my own bag of ingredients a glance. "Besides, I'm sure you've got some spectacular recipe to make."

"Dad's Dutch apple pie," I admitted. "But your gingerbread sounds really good. I wasn't sure you'd—" I cut myself off, suddenly realizing that in his current mood, Mac might not take what I was about to say particularly well.

"You didn't think I'd have a family recipe, did you," Mac said, finishing the thought for me. "Poor Mac, with his mean dad, no mum, violent brother and horrible home life that made him start burning things down."

"That's not what I... Look, I'm sorry. I am. But—"

Mac shook his head. "You don't get it at all, do you? They're my family. It's my life. And, yeah, maybe it's not perfect, but it's not all bad, either. We have good times. I had a grandma who baked with me when I was little. I like working at the garage, even if it's not what I want to do forever. I don't need you – or anyone – to save me from my life."

The worst part was, he didn't even sound really angry. More like I was never going to understand. Would never be able to be a part of his life.

But he was wrong. I did understand. "You needed help and you weren't going to ask for it, so I did it for you. Because you're my friend and I care about you and, yeah, maybe you like your family and the garage and everything – but that's not all you want. And I want you to have everything you want."

I couldn't tell him it wasn't just for him. But I wasn't lying, either. Mac's happiness was important to me. I couldn't say when it had happened, or why, but I wanted him to succeed. I wanted him to prove everybody wrong.

Especially Mrs Tyler.

Mac stared at me for a moment, like he couldn't believe someone as stupid as me actually existed. Then Miss Anderson was suddenly standing beside our station, looking pointedly at our unopened ingredients. "How's everything going here?"

Baking. Right. I knew there was a reason we were there.

"We're just discussing our recipes," I said, smiling as convincingly as I could.

"Well, you might want to start making them," Miss Anderson said, "if you want any chance of finishing them by the time I have to kick you all out."

"Of course," I said, and opened my bag. By the time I looked across at Mac again, he had his ingredients in order on the other side of the counter and was already stirring something on the hob. Guess our talking time was over.

My pie took longer to bake than the others, something I'd forgotten when I chose it. Still, it meant I got to go round and taste everyone else's. Yasmin had made some incredible Indian sweets that her sister-in-law had taught her the recipe for, while Jasper had baked a delicious coffee and walnut cake from his nan's recipe. Ella had made scones, loaded with jam and cream, and Grace a tray of delicate lemon biscuits.

I didn't ask for a piece of Mac's gingerbread.

As everyone's timers started to go off, Miss Anderson said, "Once they're ready, everyone bring their bakes to the main table."

She waited until mine was finally ready, although still too hot to eat, and then called us all over to sit down at the table. Mac chose a seat at the opposite end to me, but I could still see his gingerbread. It was a cake, rather than a biscuit, and it looked moist, sticky and delicious.

Then the door opened and a man walked in dressed in a white chef's jacket emblazoned with the logo of a local bakery. "Am I late?" he asked.

Miss Anderson turned to smile at him. "Not at all. We're just ready for you."

The baker rubbed his hands together. "Great. I'm starving."

"Guys, this is Julien," Miss Anderson said. "He owns the White Hill Bakery in town."

"Have any of you ever been there?" Julien asked, and we all nodded. Selling everything from artisan French cakes to British pasties to speciality breads, the White Hill Bakery had caused quite a stir when it opened a couple of years ago.

"Julien's here to taste your bakes today," Miss Anderson said. "So I'll let you explain to him what they are."

He started with Grace, praising the crispness of her biscuits. He enjoyed the icing on Jasper's coffee cake, which was obviously miles better than the original cake-mix icing he'd made in the first couple of weeks. Ella's scones went down well, and Yasmin's Indian sweets even better.

"I've never tasted anything quite like them," Julien said, reaching for a second. "Family recipe?"

Yasmin tilted her head. "Sort of. It's from my sister-in-law's family. She taught me to make them over the holidays." She grinned. "The food's the best part of living in such a crowded house."

I held my breath as he moved on to Mac's gingerbread. "The depth of flavour is fantastic,"

Julien said, looking at Mac with interest. "Almost savoury. I like it."

Mac just ducked his head.

"And what's this?" Julien asked, reaching me at last. "Is it cool enough now?"

"Should be. It's my dad's recipe for Dutch apple pie." I cut him a slice. "It has a pastry base, apple pie filling and a crumble top."

Julien took a bite, and nodded his approval as he swallowed. "It's good. They're all good." He turned to Miss Anderson with a smile. "You have a talented bunch of bakers here. How about you bring them to my bakery one day to see exactly what a baker does all day long?"

"What do you think, guys?" Miss Anderson asked. "Sound like fun?"

We all agreed that it did. Even Mac. When I looked over at him, he looked happier than he had all day, but when he spotted me, his face dropped. Was he ever going to forgive me?

Mac and I cleared up in silence. I could hear the others chatting about the work-experience day over dirty dishes, and Grace complaining that Yasmin washed up wrong, always using too much washing-up liquid. But Mac and I didn't say a word and, as the last dish was put away, he hung up his tea towel to dry and walked out without saying goodbye.

I stared after him, blinking fast to stop any tears of frustration. I'd said what I had to, now it was his turn.

"Hang on, Mac." Miss Anderson broke off her conversation with Julien just as Mac reached the door and he paused, turning on his heel to face her, his expression sullen. "Just before you go, I've got something new for you all to try next week. Something you might want to get some practice in for between now and next Thursday."

Mac glared at me. I ignored him. "What is it?" I asked instead.

"A technical challenge," Miss Anderson said, a wicked smile on her lips. "Just like in the competition."

"Sounds … challenging," Jasper said. "What are we making?"

"A British classic." Miss Anderson pulled a stack of laminated recipes out of her desk drawer. "Bakewell tart."

Jasper passed out the recipes, and I read through mine immediately. I'd never made a Bakewell tart before, but I liked the sound of a challenge.

"I'll leave you to absorb that while I show Julien out," Miss Anderson said.

The moment the door closed behind them, Grace said, "So… Saturday at mine again? Ten o'clock?"

"Definitely," Yasmin said, eyes fixed on the recipe.

"Me too," Ella added.

"Count me in." Jasper looked across the room at Mac. "You in?"

For a moment, I thought he'd leave without answering. But then he nodded, a short, jerky movement that I hoped we could take as a "yes".

Looked like I'd get another chance that week to put things right between us. Or convince him he was an idiot.

Either worked fine for me.

BAKEWELL TART

1. To make the pastry, tip 150g of plain flour, 75g of cold, diced butter, a pinch of salt and 25g of caster sugar into a bowl and rub together with fingertips until the mixture resembles breadcrumbs. (Alternatively, use a food processor to do this.)

2. Add an egg yolk and 1 tsp of cold water and mix until the dough comes together.

3. Flatten the dough into a disc, cover with clingfilm and chill for 30 minutes.

4. Roll out the pastry on a lightly floured surface to about 3mm thickness.

5. Line a 20-cm fluted tart tin with the pastry and prick the base with a fork.

6. Chill for another 20 minutes.

7. Heat the oven to 180°C/fan 160°C/gas 4.

8. Bake blind for about 20 minutes until the pastry is a pale golden colour.

9. Brush the inside of the pastry case with a little egg white and cook for a further 2 minutes. Cool slightly.

10. Spread 2–3 tbsp of raspberry jam in an even layer over the base of the pastry case.

11. Cream together 150g of butter and 150g of caster sugar, then gradually add 3 beaten eggs plus one egg yolk.

12. Fold in 150g ground almonds and the zest of a lemon.

13. Carefully spoon the mixture over the jam and spread level.

14. Bake for 20 minutes.

15. Scatter with 1 tbsp of flaked almonds and continue to cook for a further 15 to 20 minutes until golden and set.

16. Cool to room temperature, dust with icing sugar and serve with pouring cream or custard.

When I arrived at Grace's house on Saturday, late so I wouldn't have to be the first one there, there was no sign of Mac. But just as I finished unpacking all the ingredients for the practice tarts, the doorbell finally rang.

"I'll get it," I said, even though it wasn't my house, I wasn't closest to the door and I was the only person actually doing something else. Nobody tried to stop me, although I did catch Grace rolling her eyes.

When I opened the door, Mac stood on the other side, his jacket open to show an oil-stained T-shirt below. The nerves I'd felt all morning kicked up a gear. For a long moment we just looked at each other, until he raised an eyebrow and said, "Can I come in?"

I stood aside to let him pass. "You're late."

"Got held up at the garage. Did you start without me?"

"Not yet." I paused. "I'm glad you came, though. We all need to practise together."

"So you've said. To everyone."

"Oh, for—"

Mac looked at me in surprise, and I cut off a curse, huffing out a breath instead. "Look, I'm sorry! I said I'm sorry. I get it, I do. Your secret, not mine. But you have to at least admit I was trying to help."

Shrugging off his jacket, Mac hung it on the ornate banister at the bottom of the stairs, where it looked totally out of place. I couldn't help but remember the last time we'd stood in the shadow of this staircase. We'd been closer then, so close I could feel his breath. But this time the metre or so between us felt like miles.

"I know you were doing what you thought was best," Mac said eventually. "That you were doing it for me. I just..." He stopped, and turned to lean against the staircase. At least this way he was actually looking at me. "People always think they know everything about me, right? They know my record and think that says it all."

"Not me," I said quietly, and was rewarded with the first smile he'd given me since I asked Grace to let us bake there.

"No," he said. "Not you. Which is why ... I guess that's why I lost it. I thought you knew me better."

"I do. I know you want to bake." He flinched.

"Why don't you want anyone else to know that?" I asked, frustrated. "Because the guys you hang around with wouldn't approve?"

"No!" He reached out, his hand resting on my arm. "I don't care what they think. I've never cared what anyone thinks."

"Then what?"

Mac drew in a long breath before answering. "I just… If they knew it mattered to me…"

Suddenly it all clicked into place in my head and I finished his thought, "Then they could take it away."

"Yeah." His head dropped, eyes on the floor, and I moved closer, just to try and get him to look at me again. "Right now, the school still thinks this baking thing is a punishment. If someone tells them it's … well, not … next time I screw up, they'll kick me out of the group for sure."

I tensed.

"So we won't tell them. Nobody here would, anyway. They're all your friends. Even Grace." As much as it pained me to admit it.

"I know." His voice was soft. "I know."

"And I'm your friend." More than a friend, maybe, if he'd let me be.

He looked up and the brightness of his eyes made my heart catch all over again. "Just my friend?"

I didn't think about it too much. If I had, I'd have talked myself out of it before I even moved. Instead, I rose up on my tiptoes, one hand against his chest, and pressed my lips against his.

Everything else ceased to matter for as long as we were kissing. All thoughts of baking, of competitions, of the others in the kitchen, even of my mum, or his dad – they all floated away. All I could think about was the way his hands felt at my waist, all I could feel was his breath mingling with mine. All I could care about was that moment, just the two of us.

But eventually the real world intruded, in the form of Jasper opening the kitchen door, saying, "Oh! Sorry!" very loudly, and slamming the door again. The sound of laughter soon followed from behind it.

I pulled away, dropping back down to my normal height, and trying not to blush as I looked up at Mac.

"So... not just a friend?" he said, after a moment.

"Not just a friend." Now it was my turn to look at my feet, but Mac's quick fingers caught my chin and kept me looking at him.

"So?"

"So we're ... more than friends?" I had no idea what else to call it. Guys like Mac didn't date girls like me. He might have learned to love baking, made friends with Jasper and Ella and me… But even with everything I'd learned about him over the last few months, I couldn't imagine for a moment walking into school on Monday as Mac's girlfriend. And I dreaded to think about what Mrs Tyler would say once word got around!

Mac's smile was slow but warm. "More than friends. Sounds good."

For a long moment, I could do nothing but smile back at him. But eventually, the sounds from the kitchen became too loud to ignore and it was time to return to the real world.

"Think they're talking about us in there?" I asked.

"Oh yeah," Mac said, with the kind of indifference that only someone who genuinely didn't care could manage.

I wasn't there yet. "We should head back in."

"We should, probably," Mac said.

But he kissed me again before we went.

Back in the kitchen, Grace was holding court. "As I was explaining to those people who weren't otherwise occupied in my hallway," she said as we entered, "since you've all taken over my kitchen, I've volunteered you for something in return."

Mac leaned against the kitchen counter and pulled me in to lean against him. I couldn't help the way my muscles tensed at the sensation of him behind me. I knew that these people didn't care and hadn't I just told Mac that they were our friends? We were together now. Sort of.

"Volunteered?" Jasper asked. "Don't we have to *offer* to help for it to be volunteering?"

Ella asked, "What will we be doing?"

"Making and serving the interval refreshments for the school play." Grace said, her eyes innocent.

"While you star in it," Jasper said. "Our dream."

His sarcasm didn't seem to register with Grace, though.

"Well, obviously I'll be busy."

"When is it, anyway?" Ella pulled her diary out of her bag. "I'm away visiting Mum in a couple of weeks."

Jasper's face turned dark at that, but Grace didn't seem to notice. "It's the week after half-term," she said. "Fourth of March."

Of course. My birthday. What else could I have asked for on my special day but to watch Grace prance round as queen of the fairies in front of an adoring crowd?

But, actually, there was another issue. "That's the week of the competition," I pointed out. "We'll need to be practising for that."

Grace shrugged, an elegant rise of the shoulders. "So use this as practice."

"We can do that," Yasmin said, unerringly cheery. "It'll be a great opportunity to try out our group bakes before the big day."

I'd been outmanoeuvred, it seemed. Pulling away from Mac, I said, "Speaking of which … shouldn't we be getting on with this?" I motioned to the pile of ingredients on the counter.

Behind me, Mac stepped up. "OK, then. Where do we start?"

"Weighing, measuring and putting things in order."

Mac slapped a hand against his forehead. "Of course."

It took us quite a few tries to make a Miss Anderson-worthy Bakewell tart, and even then we weren't a hundred per cent sure how we managed it. Mac handled the shortcrust pastry for the first one and we remembered enough of the asparagus quiche recipe from the week before to cope when the recipe said merely, "bake blind". Not letting the jam and filling mix was an issue, but we got there in the end. And by the late afternoon we all had a reasonable grasp of what we were going to have to do on Thursday, which was more than we usually had.

Mac kissed me goodbye on the doorstep with everyone watching and, for once, I managed to just let go and enjoy it without worrying about what the others were saying. So by the time I turned into Orchard Avenue, I was in a pretty good mood.

Until I saw Mrs Robertson from number thirty-eight hammering on our front door.

I dashed through the gate to try and intercept her. "Mrs Robertson! I don't think Mum is home right now..."

"I know she's in there," Mrs Robertson said, banging one last time on the door for good measure. "I've been watching. She's not gone out this morning."

"Maybe she went out through the back gate?" I said, trying not to wince at the lie.

"How could she?" Mrs Robertson asked. "With your back garden so full of ... of rubbish! That's why I'm here. This has gone on long enough!"

"Mrs Robertson, I'm sure you understand that it's been difficult for Mum and me, keeping on top of the garden maintenance, as well as everything else, since Dad died." Part of me hated using the "dead dad" card for sympathy, but a larger part just wanted Mrs Robertson to go away before anyone else came out to see what was going on.

For once, though, the sympathy ploy didn't work. "I dare say it has," Mrs Robertson said. "But eventually you've got to pick yourself up and start again. That garden is a health hazard and by rights I should contact the council. And if it's an indication of what's inside…" She shuddered and I only just managed to resist doing so myself.

The council. I hadn't even thought about the council, I'd been so busy focusing on keeping the school away.

"I'll talk to Mum," I promised. "We'll get it sorted. Hire a skip, if we need to. Just … don't call anyone. I'll fix it."

Mrs Robertson's eyes softened as she looked at me. "It's not you that should have to, love. You're just a girl."

"Mum will help. As soon as she gets back from … wherever she is."

"If you say so." Mrs Robertson turned to go, her eyes sad. But at the gate, she paused. "If you need anything. Any help. You can always ask, you know."

"I know," I said. But I wouldn't. We both knew that too.

I waited until Mrs Robertson was safely back in her own house before I opened the front door, pretending to busy myself with a pot of dead bulbs by the step. I couldn't risk her glimpsing the hallway beyond. If she thought the back garden was bad...

I found Mum in her room, as usual. I didn't even ask why she hadn't answered the door; she never did any more.

"Mrs Robertson came by," was all I said. "She's concerned about our back garden."

Mum actually looked surprised. "Really? Why?"

"She thinks it's a health hazard."

"That woman," Mum said, her face a picture of indignation. "What right has she?"

I sighed. "She's threatening to call the council, Mum. We have to clear it."

"But those are my things. I might need them."

"The council will just throw them all away." I didn't know if that was true, but it seemed like a winning argument. "If we sort it, we could go through everything. Keep the most important things and get rid of the rest."

Mum considered it for a moment, then waved a dismissive hand. "It'll all have to come inside."

"But where, Mum?" I asked, despairing. "There's no room left."

Her eyes took on a glimmer of hope as she looked at me. "There's your room."

"No." Not a chance. My room was the only space I had that wasn't a shrine to Stuff. And it was staying that way.

"Then it will have to stay in the back garden," Mum said, with the perfectly flawed logic of someone who thinks they've won an argument they don't even understand.

"It can't, Mum."

"Then you'll need to think of somewhere else to put it." And with that, she turned back to her TV.

Discussion over.

BRIOCHE

1. Rub 100g of butter into 250g of plain flour, then stir in 50g of caster sugar, 1 tsp of salt and 7g of fast-action yeast.
2. Add 3 eggs and mix to form a soft dough.
3. Cover and chill for 20 minutes, then knead on a floured surface for 5 minutes.
4. Drop into a greased 900g loaf tin, cover with clingfilm and leave to rise for around 2 hours, or until doubled in size.
5. Heat the oven to 200°C/fan 180°C/gas 6.
6. Brush the top of the brioche with egg yolk, then sprinkle over a little sugar and bake for 20 to 25 minutes, until golden brown.
7. If the loaf sounds hollow when tapped, it's done.
8. Tip out on to a wire rack and leave to cool.

The week before half-term, the whole Bake Club traipsed down to the White Hill Bakery for our work-experience day. At five in the morning.

As it turned out, the only one of us who was any good at stupidly early starts was Mac.

"How are you so awake?" I asked, as he handed me a cardboard cup full of hot, sweet tea.

Mac just shrugged. "The garage opens at seven-thirty on weekdays to let people get their cars in before work. Dad likes us there an hour before to get things set up and jobs finished. This isn't that much earlier."

I frowned. "Do you work there every morning?"

"Most, I suppose." He flashed me a grin. "Where else would I get the money to buy you tea? Besides, I'm making it up to Jamie for all the hours I'm missing for Bake Club."

Which meant he was working for hours before he even came to school. I knew Mac hated anyone feeling sorry for him, but still, I couldn't help it.

Julien was waiting for us when we arrived, standing in the doorway with a mug in hand.

"Welcome to the White Hill Bakery," he said, spreading out his arms. "Here we make real food from real ingredients, with real heart. You guys might have baked before, but here, you'll become bakers."

He slapped his hands against his apron, sending a small puff of flour up into the air. "Also it's bloody hard work. So let's get started!"

He led us all through the main shop to the kitchens at the back. "Croissant dough has finished rising, so you," he pointed at Grace, "go and help Marie get the croissants in the ovens and start on the puff pastry for today's slices and pasties. Then you'll be making tomorrow's croissants."

Grace hurried off in the direction he indicated, where she joined a smiling brunette, whose hands were already caked in flour.

"OK, next, you and you." I stopped staring after the others and paid attention as he pointed at me and Jasper. "You're helping Tom with the morning goods – macaroons, éclairs and doughnuts. Off you go."

I glanced back at Mac as I trailed off after Jasper. Yasmin was already being sent in the direction of the bread ovens, with instructions about loaves of white bread. But Julien was keeping Mac with him. I wondered what he had planned.

"What's with the normality today?" I asked Jasper, as we injected strawberry jam into the centre of the doughnuts. Not only was his hair still blond, but his clothes were downright plain.

Jasper glanced down at his blue jeans and faded green T-shirt. "It was four in the morning, Lottie. I just grabbed whatever was at the bottom of my wardrobe."

"What do your parents think of the new you?" To me, it looked like he'd lost the will to even bother trying to confuse them. Maybe things with Ella were a higher priority to him. Except Ella wasn't even here today.

Jasper pulled a face. "Dunno. They haven't really said anything. They just keep smiling at each other. Like they've succeeded in making me normal again."

As if Jasper was ever going to be normal. Besides, couldn't they see that not caring what he looked like was much more worrying in Jasper than Gothing it up?

"How's Ella?"

Another face. "Haven't spoken to her since she left with her mum on Monday."

"Oh." I didn't bother trying to interpret Ella's

silence for him; I was sure he'd been through all the possibilities himself in the last few days. Basically it came down to: her mum didn't want her talking to him, or she was having too good a time up north to even think about him. Neither of which boded well.

The morning goods kept us busy for the next hour or so, by which point it was time to move on to sausage rolls and pasties. Julien kept us all moving, shifting us from one spot in the bakery to another, letting us try our hand at all sorts of different treats.

He also insisted we each did a stint on the counter, so that we "experienced all aspects of life in a bakery". It wasn't going to be much help in the competition, but I could see his point, so I didn't grumble.

At least, until Mrs Robertson came in for her morning loaf of bread.

My first instinct was panic, my heart thumping double time as I watched her push open the bakery door. My feet felt welded to the ground, like the heavy bread ovens in the back kitchens. What would she say? I hadn't had time to clear more than a few things from the back garden. Everything was sodden, anyway, wet through from the horrible weather we'd had all week. It all needed dumping, but I couldn't afford a skip on my pocket money and Mum clearly wasn't going to help.

What if she'd called the council already? What if she'd come here to tell me, in front of all my friends, Julien, the bakery staff and customers, that the council were going to come and clear my house for us? That I was going to be taken into care? That Mum might end up in some sort of institution for the clinically possessive?

Every one of those thoughts rushed through my mind in the time it took Mrs Robertson to open the door.

And then sanity, followed by survival instinct, kicked in. She wasn't here for me. She was here for bread, that was all. Me being here was just a coincidence.

Which meant she wouldn't miss me if she didn't see me.

Smiling at the customer I was meant to be serving, I said, "Let me just check the back," and ducked into the bakery kitchen, my heart still hammering. Behind me, I could hear the customer calling, "Uh, miss? There's one right here…" but I ignored them.

"Customer service not really your thing?" Mac asked and when I looked up, I realized that my hiding place was only a metre or so from where he was kneading dough.

A good lie always has an element of truth,

I remembered. "Evil neighbour just came in," I said. "When I was twelve, she complained so much about my cat using her garden as a toilet that we had to give it away." All true. Just not why I was hiding from her.

"Fair enough," Mac said, taking my story at face value.

I let out a breath, my heart starting to work at something approaching normal speed again. "What are you making?"

"Brioche." Mac turned the dough and pushed it away from him again. "Apparently Miss Anderson told Julien I like breads. So he wants me to learn to make some of his speciality loaves."

"That's great!" For a moment, I forgot about Mrs Robertson. "None of the rest of us have made any breads. And a speciality one will look great with the judges."

Mac kept staring at the dough, as his hands worked it, making it pliable. "Yeah. Doubt there'll be much time in the competition, though."

I realized he hadn't been thinking about the competition. He was thinking about his future. "Maybe Julien has a part-time job available," I said.

Mac shook his head. "No go, even if he did. I couldn't do this and the garage. Besides, who'd pay me to make bread?"

"One day, maybe all sorts of people."

"But not right now," Mac said. "Too much to learn."

The door to the counter area of the bakery flew open and Tina, the girl who'd been showing me how to use the cash register, scowled through the doorway. "When you've quite finished flirting, I could do with some help out here."

I sidled up to the door and peered through, just in time to see the back of Mrs Robertson's coat as she left. "Absolutely," I said brightly. "Sorry about that."

Disaster averted. For now.

By the time the bakery closed its doors at five-thirty that afternoon, we were all beyond exhausted. Three different shifts of bakers had come in throughout the day, some starting as early as three that morning, but only Julien had been there the full day. And as we hit the twelve-hour point, we were ready to go home.

"Don't worry," Julien said, as Tina flipped the sign over to closed and locked the door. "I won't make you stay and clear-up. This time."

We groaned at that, but actually, the idea of a next time was encouraging.

"They didn't do too badly, then?" Miss Anderson asked. She'd stopped by after school to see how we were getting on and ended up helping out with the bread dough for the following day. Julien had smiled at her. A lot.

Julien grinned at her again. "Actually, they did a great job. I see real potential here." He gave Jasper, who was draped over the counter half-asleep, a prod in the shoulder blades. He barely flinched. "Once they build up their stamina, anyway."

"So you think you could bear to come in now and then to taste their bakes? Maybe give them some pointers?" Miss Anderson beamed around the bakery at us all.

"I think I can do better than that, actually," Julien said. "In France, where my father's family ran a bakery, they always had an apprentice – someone to train up and teach the special recipes to. I was one, as was my cousin, who now runs our sister bakery in Paris. So when I started the White Hill Bakery, here in the country where I grew up, I knew I wanted to take on apprentices too." He leaned against the counter as he looked us over. "Here's my proposal. In two months' time, you will all bake for me. Cake, bread, pie, whatever you choose. And whoever I judge to have made the best bake will spend the summer as my apprentice. Five weeks here and, if your parents agree and your lovely teacher will chaperone, one week in Paris."

Paris. A real bakery. A grin spread across my face and, when I looked around, everyone else was smiling too. This was more than a competition, this was a chance at a future. Real baking, more than I'd ever learned from Dad, or at Bake Club. And Paris! A whole week away, trying new foods, learning new techniques... I wanted it so much it burned.

Miss Anderson didn't look surprised at the announcement and I realized she had already known what Julien was planning. Were they dating? Was this Julien's way of winning brownie points with her?

Really, I didn't care why he was doing it. All I wanted was the opportunity.

But, I realized, I wasn't the only one.

Grace and Yasmin were chattering at rapid speed in the corner, and I knew it had to be about Paris. Even Jasper had perked up at the announcement, and was looking over the half-empty bakery cases, as if for inspiration.

And Mac... Mac looked, just for a moment, like he'd been thrown a lifeline. He stared at Julien as if he had the capacity to make all his dreams come true.

Guilt set in. Mac did need this. And he didn't even know why I needed it too. A chance to bake, all summer, without dealing with his dad, or the

Stuff... Of course we both wanted it. And we were going to have to fight each other to get it.

Suddenly, the whole idea sucked.

I liked Mac. I cared about Mac. I wanted Mac to have the future he wanted.

But I couldn't give up my own future to give it to him.

He'd understand that. Wouldn't he?

"What do you think?" I asked, moving to his side. "You want it, I bet."

Mac shrugged. "Not really."

I looked at him in disbelief. "Why not?" Because I was bored of macho pretending-I-don't-want-what-I-obviously-do Mac.

"I'll be working at the garage this summer, anyway," he said, like it was written in stone somewhere.

"But instead, you could be working at the bakery."

Mac shook his head. "No. If, against all the odds, Julien picked me, I could get up every morning and knead dough, for little to no money. And then be unemployed and probably homeless in September when I have to start sixth form or college."

"Your dad would kick you out for baking?" Maybe Mac did have bigger problems than me. My mum would never kick me out. Unless it meant she could use my room to store more Stuff, of course. That was always a possibility.

"If I'm not working at the garage or studying to be a proper mechanic, I'm not contributing to the family," Mac said. "I have to 'earn my place' in the house." He was quoting his dad there, I was sure.

"So, you get a flat somewhere and study baking instead. You weren't planning on living at home your whole life anyway, right?"

"With what money? You remember the unpaid apprenticeship thing, right? Not to mention the lack of a job in September. And anyway, I don't think I even need to worry about it." Mac picked up a plastic teaspoon from a pot on the counter and started running it between his fingers. "You'll win it anyway. You're the best baker in the group."

"That's not true."

Mac raised a disbelieving eyebrow. "They're not listening, you know. You don't need to be all fake-modest with me."

"I'm not!" I tried to find a way to explain. "When we started, I knew more than most of you, because my dad had taught me. But now, you're all catching up. Yasmin and Grace are cooking all the time at home, Ella and Jasper have been discussing new recipes to try and develop for the competition. And

Julien taught you how to make his famous brioche loaf."

"Still. You've got a feel for it."

"So have you." I looked up into his eyes. "You could be really great at this, Mac. And it could be a big chance for you. Don't give up on it just yet."

Mac gave me a lopsided smile. "Maybe."

And just like that, I felt my heart crack a little. Because I'd done just what I said I wouldn't. I'd started to give up on my dream to encourage his.

BIRTHDAY CAKE

1. Make a traditional sponge sandwich (see Classic Victoria Sandwich recipe, p.42) substituting 25g of flour for cocoa.
2. For the icing, combine 75g of granulated sugar and 95ml of evaporated milk in a heavy saucepan and put on a low heat, stirring until all the sugar has dissolved.
3. Bring to the boil and simmer gently for exactly 6 minutes without stirring.
4. Take the pan off the heat and stir in 100g of dark chocolate, broken into pieces, until it has all melted.
5. Stir in 40g butter and 2 drops of vanilla extract.
6. Transfer to a bowl, cool and cover with clingfilm.
7. Chill for a couple of hours until it has thickened enough to spread between the cakes, and on top.

When I was little, first thing on the morning of my birthday, Dad would bounce into my room with arms full of presents and a cupcake with a candle in it. He'd light it, and he and Mum would sing "Happy Birthday" to me, and I'd be allowed to eat the cake for breakfast.

Last year, Mum forgot my birthday altogether, until I reminded her at dinnertime. I suppose I should have been grateful that she remembered my sixteenth at all.

I wasn't, particularly.

At six-thirty that morning she threw open my bedroom door, sang very loudly as I hid under the covers, and then presented me with a basket full of things wrapped in newspaper.

"What's this?" I asked, reluctantly sitting up and slumping against the headboard.

"Your presents." Mum perched on the corner of my mattress. Despite the early hour, I felt a small stirring of excitement. Not only had she remembered, she'd made an effort to celebrate. Maybe she was finally moving out of the depression that had sunk her since Dad died. Maybe she'd be ready to join the real, normal world again. The one where people didn't have piles of Stuff all the way up the stairs.

But then I opened the basket. "Um... I don't know what to say." What *do* you say when your mother presents you with, in order, some old shoes (wrong size), two mismatched tea cups (chipped), a Beano annual from 1979 (puzzles completed) and three cassette tapes of 1980s workout music?

Mum picked up one of the tapes. "Do you like them? We'll need to dig out the cassette recorder. I'm sure it's up here somewhere."

"You threw it out years ago," I said, without thinking.

Mum's face went blank. "I'll buy a new one, then. I'll head down to the charity shop today."

Great. More Stuff to go with the charity-shop birthday presents and the Stuff going mouldy in the back garden.

Best birthday ever.

That evening the school hall was all set up for the play, with chairs in rows from the stage to the back doors. I couldn't imagine there were really that many people who'd want to see it, but Grace seemed convinced. Either way, it meant that we were shoved in the room off to the side, with our trestle tables and makeshift tablecloths stolen from the costume department. Grace wanted themed food for the audience, so we were serving fairy cakes (obviously) with little butterfly wings and silver sparkles, butter biscuits with purple icing and silver edible glitter, and a non-alcoholic "Love Potion", or berry punch.

As we finally loaded the last lot of cakes on to trays in the food tech classroom, ready to cart them over to the hall, Ella caught my arm. "Wait a minute," she said, and I nodded, as Jasper and Yasmin disappeared through the doors. Grace was off preparing for the show and Mac hadn't even arrived yet, so Ella and I were alone.

"What's up?" I asked, perching on the large table in the centre of the room. "Is it your gran?"

Ella shook her head. "No, no. Gran's... Well, she's not fine. But she's OK. And Dad's here, which helps. No. It's..."

She trailed off, so I finished the thought for her. If it wasn't her family, it had to be, "Jasper."

Ella nodded miserably. "I don't know what to say to him! He's convinced I want to leave and of course

I don't, but I might not have any choice."

"It's looking that likely?" God, Jasper was going to be heartbroken if Ella moved. I'd hardly seen them apart since Christmas. Yasmin and I had even tried coming up with a couple-name for them, one boring lunchtime, 'Elsper' being the best we'd managed.

Looked like we wouldn't need it now.

"Mum wants me with her. She always did, really. But when she first moved up north it wasn't practical. But now she's all settled, and with Dad away so much, there aren't any other options."

"What about school?"

"Mum's got me a place at the local one up there already."

"But there's got to be something we can do!" I searched for an answer. "What about—"

"There isn't, Lottie. Don't you think I've tried? Unless Dad manages to work something out..."

We sat there in depressed silence until suddenly I realized something. Jasper had been back in his Goth gear that afternoon. Not at lunchtime, but by after school he'd reclaimed his black hoodie and the eyeliner. His hair was still blond, and we'd been so busy I'd barely noticed.

"How did your mum like Jasper?" I asked.

Ella raised a shoulder in a half-shrug. "She said

he seemed nice enough, but that long-distance relationships never work out."

Ah. That might explain it. "You told Jasper that?"

Ella's face crumpled. "He asked! And I didn't say I believed it! But he just disappeared off to lessons without saying anything."

Boys. So stupid. "He's probably just trying to figure it all out in his head." Or, more likely, trying to put distance between them so it didn't hurt so much when she had to go.

Ella sighed and slumped against the table next to me. "I just don't know what to do."

Awkwardly, I put an arm round her shoulders, patting her school jumper in what I hoped was a comforting manner. "Seems to me there's not much you can do. Tonight's going to be crazy enough as it is. Let him work it out and you can talk tomorrow."

"Maybe," Ella said, in the sort of way that suggested she was going to ignore everything I'd just said and hunt Jasper down for answers immediately.

Yasmin, it turned out, was definitely the hostess of our group. Maybe if Grace hadn't been so busy with the play, she'd have had to fight for the role. But as it was, from the moment Grace had announced that we'd be providing the refreshments for the play,

Yasmin had gone into planning mode. She'd come up with a timetable for the day's baking and had scoured the internet for examples of *A Midsummer Night's Dream*-themed parties.

When Ella and I reached the little side room where we were doing the catering, Yasmin was already bossing everyone about. I'd always thought she was happy to go along with what everyone else wanted, but apparently that disappeared when she set her mind on creating the perfect event.

"Jasper, don't put those cakes there, they clash with the biscuits. Move them to the other side of the glasses." She squinted at the table as Jasper shifted things round. "No. That doesn't work, either. Try them over this side."

I drifted away from the table, not wanting to get dragged in for an opinion on clashing cakes, but Yasmin spotted me. "Lottie! Great. I need you to get on with the decorations for the entrance."

I've never had any ambition to be an interior designer. But still, as I finished stringing fairy lights over the gold and blue fabric we'd used to make a draping curtain in the doorway from the hall, I had to admit that between us all we'd done a great job.

The first of the audience started trickling into

the hall as I reached for the last strand of battery-powered fairy lights. Shifting my chair across to the other side of the curtain, I climbed back up and tried to reach high enough to pin them in place. Thanks to a badly placed radiator, I couldn't quite get close enough, even when I tried leaning further and further over.

Maybe if I stood on the radiator itself...

I placed my foot on the metal, but the chair began to creep backwards on the block-wood floor, screeching against the varnish. *Damn it!* I grabbed for something to cling on to, but the only thing in reach was the curtain, and even as my fingers closed round the slippery fabric, I knew it wouldn't hold me.

Icy fear shot through me as I flailed around, trying to find something to stop me falling. All I could think was, *This is going to hurt...*

But then, two strong hands wrapped round my waist, steadying me on the wobbling chair. The plastic seat stopped moving, and when I glanced down, my breath fast and shallow, I saw that it was held in place by a foot. Attached to a leg. Belonging to a body with a ridiculously good-looking face above it.

Mac.

"My hero," I said, when my heart had stopped thumping against my ribcage. I said it like a joke, like

I'd have been fine, but honestly I meant it. "I didn't think you were going to make it tonight."

Carefully, Mac helped me down from the chair, his hands never moving from my body, as if he was scared to let me go. "And miss you trying to break your head open? Never."

"You missed all the baking," I pointed out.

He gave me a sheepish look. "Sorry about that. I was rostered on at the garage after school and Jamie couldn't cover for me. I got here as quickly as I could."

"Just in time, by the look of it," Mr Carroll said from behind me.

I stepped back so quickly I almost fell again, even though I was standing on solid ground this time.

"Um, I should try and get this last set of lights up," I said, as Mac gave me a weird look. "The audience is already coming in."

"I'll do it," Mac said, taking the lights from me.

Mr Carroll looked from Mac to me. "Probably a good idea. Careful up there, Mr Macintyre." He walked away, through the curtain and into the main hall.

Mac clambered up on to the chair. I watched for a moment, but he didn't look down at me or speak to me. And then, when he was done, he stepped down and headed straight over to Yasmin, asking, "What can I do next?"

Mr Carroll had ruined another perfect moment.

"Did you two fall out again?" Jasper asked, in between handing over cups of tea. "Because this on-again, off-again thing is confusing. I like to work in definites."

"I just don't like teachers knowing my business. And anyway, you can't talk." I licked the icing off a slightly misshapen biscuit that wasn't good enough to put out. "What's going on with you and Ella? She's worried."

Jasper reached for a cupcake. The queue had finally calmed down, and I could hear Mr Carroll calling for the audience to take their seats.

"Not much point anything going on with me and Ella, is there?" Jasper said.

"She might not move," I tried, but it didn't sound very convincing, even to me.

Jasper sighed. "Even if she doesn't, it just made me think. She'd rather keep her family happy than be with me. Which I get, I suppose. She's missed her mum since she moved away. I know that. It's just…"

"You wanted a grand, epic love for the ages?"

"Nah, I'll leave that for you and Mac." He nudged

me in the ribs. "Bad boy crosses the tracks to be with grade-A student, and even learns to bake to prove his love."

"Doesn't sound particularly familiar," I said drily. "More, girl with slipping grades teaches bad boy to bake, and then he takes pity on her and kisses her."

Jasper's eyebrows sank down in a concerned look. "You don't really think that, do you? He's crazy about you. Everyone can see that."

Could they? Because I … I wanted to. But it was hard to trust my instincts. Hard to trust that he'd feel the same, if he knew the truth. "Everyone except me, then."

"Probably." He smiled. "For all your OCD tendencies, you're not the most observant of people, you know."

"I don't have OCD."

Jasper laughed, too loud, and got shushed by Yasmin, who was watching the play through the curtain.

"Actually, I think you're slipping," Jasper whispered. "You haven't even noticed that the fairy lights are wonky. Or does it not matter because Mac put them up?"

I elbowed him back. But I couldn't help looking

up at the lights.

Definitely lopsided. Damn.

"Thanks. I'm not going to be able to look at anything else all night now."

Jasper laughed again, Yasmin glared, and even Mac looked up to raise his eyebrows at us.

Maybe things weren't quite as bad as I'd thought.

After the interval, we got started with the clearing up, shipping plates and cups back to the canteen, and the baking supplies and leftovers to the food tech classroom. By the time we were done, applause was sounding from the hall and it wasn't long before Grace came bounding in, still in full costume and sparkly make-up.

"What did you think?" she asked, grinning manically. "Wasn't it great? They messed up one of the light cues, and there was an issue with the sound, but otherwise—"

"You were wonderful," Yasmin said. Which was, of course, what Grace was waiting to hear.

She smiled down at her satin fairy slippers. "Well, obviously it was an ensemble piece."

"I loved it," Yasmin said.

"You here to help clear up?" Jasper asked. "Because we're pretty much done."

"Actually," Grace said, still smiling. "I was seeing if you guys wanted to come to the official after-show party over in the canteen. After all, you were a part of tonight."

Jasper and I looked at each other – the surprise on his face matching my thoughts.

"We'd love to!" Yasmin said, and beside her Ella nodded. Which of course meant that Jasper wiped his hands and stepped towards Ella.

"Mac?" Grace asked.

Getting to his feet, Mac made his way over to where I was standing. "I'm going to stay and help Lottie finish taking down the decorations," he said. "Maybe we'll follow on a bit later."

"Can't they wait?" Jasper asked.

"Yeah, we're not breaking down the set until tomorrow," Grace added. "I'm sure a few fairy lights won't make much of a difference."

I glanced up at Mac and he gave me an almost imperceptible shake of the head. So slight, I wasn't entirely sure of what I was seeing. But if he wanted to stay here, with me, alone…

"I'd really like to get it done now," I said, giving the others an apologetic smile. "You know me and my OCD tendencies."

Jasper rolled his eyes. "God, I bet you polish

your bed every morning once you get out of it, don't you?"

"Probably why she doesn't invite us round," Ella added, eager to get in on Jasper's joke. "Doesn't want us to mess anything up."

I forced a grin. Like they could make it any worse than it was. "Yep. You lot are far too messy for me."

"You guys go on," Mac said. "We'll see you later."

They headed out in a cloud of chatter and laughter to where the rest of the cast were waiting, all still in stage make-up.

We watched them go, and then I turned to Mac. "Are we really going to the party after?"

"Probably not." He wrapped an arm round my waist. "I've got our own party planned, right here."

"So we're not taking down fairy lights?"

"Didn't you hear Grace? They can wait until tomorrow."

Mac tugged on my hand, pulling me into the hall, then up the steps to the stage. I followed him as he ducked through the curtains, into the fairy-tale setting of *A Midsummer Night's Dream*. Like all productions at St Mary's, changing sets was a bit beyond the budget, so the stage had three areas. A central one to suggest the forest, with a palace on one side and a fairy grove on the other.

Mac led me into the forest set, sitting me down on a fake tree stump. I gave him a confused look, but he just put his finger to his lips.

A moment later, Mr Carroll called out from somewhere in the main hall, "Everybody out?"

Mac and I stared at each other in silence, my heart suddenly very loud in my chest. Moments later, the lights went out, plunging us into darkness. Then I heard the sound of doors slamming, keys turning, then … nothing.

"We're locked in here." My voice sounded incredibly calm considering the way my hands were shaking. "Is this your great plan, spending the night trapped in the school hall?" What was he thinking? And what, exactly, was he expecting to happen tonight?

Mac's chuckle came out of the blackness; even with my eyes adjusting to the dark, I couldn't see him.

I heard a match being scraped and saw the flame spark to life. "You brought matches?" I asked, wondering briefly if I should be more concerned about the arson stories than about being alone with Mac.

"I brought more than matches," Mac said, but he had his back to me now, shielding the light, and I couldn't make out more than the line of his shoulders. "Close your eyes and I'll show you."

Despite my uncertainty, I was curious. So I did as I was told.

"Open them," he said, a moment later.

As my eyes fluttered open, the first thing I saw was blobs of light. Then, as my eyes focused, I realized they were candles. Sixteen of them, stuck into the top of the most chocolatey birthday cake I'd ever seen.

"I'm not going to sing," Mac said. "But I wanted to celebrate your birthday. With you."

My breath caught in my throat as I looked at my cake. "This is why you were late, isn't it!"

Mac didn't answer, saying instead, "Aren't you going to blow them out? Make a wish and all that?"

Drawing in a deep breath, I considered my wish options. Then I blew out the flames one by one.

"What did you wish for?" Mac asked, in the darkness.

"If I tell you, it won't come true."

I felt him sit down beside me.

"Shall I tell you my wish?"

"You made a wish? It was my cake."

"Yeah, I know." His shoulder brushed against mine and he took my hand. "You want to know or not?"

"I want to know." Of course I wanted to know. What kind of question was that?

"I wished I could tell you the truth."

My heart stopped in my chest. I swear, for a moment, it actually stopped. "The truth about what?"

I felt him shrug. "Everything. About how I have these jealous feelings when we talk about the competition and the apprenticeship. Because I want you to succeed, because you deserve it, but I want to too. And how I hate that sometimes, when I look at you, all I can think about is how I want what you have. But I know I'm not that guy. Hell, I'm not even the kind of guy you want to be seen with."

My mind whirred with new information. God, if only he knew how much he *didn't* want my life.

I swallowed. "That's what you want to tell me the truth about?"

"Yeah."

"I think you just did. So your wish came true."

He chuckled and brushed my fingertips with his. "I guess it did. You mad?"

I shook my head, letting my cheek rest against his shoulder. "I get jealous too, you know. About the baking. I want you to win the apprenticeship. I want you to have everything you want. But..."

"You want it too."

"Exactly."

He kissed the top of my head. "Maybe, if we both feel like that, it's not so bad."

"I think so." Lifting my cheek, my lips grazed his jawline, then his lips, and before I knew it we were kissing again. And this time, it was deeper, stronger, and his arms were holding me closer to him than ever.

"I do want to be seen with you," I managed to murmur, between kisses. "Of course I do. I want this to be real." Just for that moment, I didn't care what Mr Carroll would say, or if he'd call my mum. Mac's kisses made me reckless.

He kissed me again. "OK then." Another kiss. "Me too. I don't want us to lie to each other." One more kiss. "I can talk to you. I don't want to lose that."

"You won't," I said fiercely. But I couldn't help thinking of all the lies I'd already told him. And how many more I'd need to tell to keep my secrets.

His hands swept up my sides, pulling me down off the log with him and into his lap. I curled up in his arms as he kissed me. My whole body felt hot, flashing with feeling and shivers and everything I'd ever read about but not really experienced. Not like this.

A clatter of metal against wood rang out and we

froze. Then Mac said, "The tin. I had the cake in a tin."

"My cake!" I scrambled off him, my mind starting to return to some sort of sanity.

Mac sat up and fumbled to light another match. "Your cake's fine," he said. He smiled up at me, his hair dishevelled and eyes bright in the match-light. "Are you?"

I nodded, smoothing down my hair. "I'm fine."

"You sure?"

"Yeah. I just..." God, could this be any more embarrassing? "I know you've, well, you've had a lot of girlfriends..."

Mac reached up and took my hand, as the match burned out. "Not like you."

I was glad he couldn't see my cheeks getting redder in the darkness. "Really?"

"Really. And this, with us... It's different for me. We don't..." he blew out a breath. Was he finding this as awkward as me? "I guess what I'm saying is, there's no hurry here. We can take this as slowly as you like."

My whole body relaxed at his words. "OK."

"OK," he repeated, squeezing my hand. "Come on. Let's break out of here and into the food tech classroom. We need a knife to cut your cake."

I reached out to find his arm and held on, following him through the darkness, and wondered when my life had become so romantic.

LEMON PIE

1. Heat the oven to 140°C/fan 120°C/gas 1.
2. Roll out 500g of shortcrust pastry to 5mm thick and line a deep 23cm-diameter tart case.
3. Prick all over with a fork and bake blind for 15 minutes.
4. Allow to cool, then brush with a beaten egg and put back in the oven for 2 minutes.
5. In a food processor, or with a hand whisk, beat 4 eggs and 200g of caster sugar.
6. Add 125ml of double cream and 175ml of lemon juice.
7. Add the zest of 2 lemons.
8. Pour into the pastry case and bake for about 35 to 40 minutes until just set.

"So wait. You were kissing on the stage and eating cake." Jasper's eyebrows were so high they had disappeared under his fringe. "That's why you didn't make the after-show party last night?"

"Kind of," I said, sinking back into the cushioned seat of the minibus and smiling to myself. "Yeah."

Across the aisle, Ella leaned across Jasper to ask, "And? What was it like?"

Jasper held up his hands. "OK, I don't need details. I just wanted to know what happened to you both."

Ella elbowed him in the ribs. "Maybe you don't. But I do! So?"

I smiled some more. "That's my business, thank you very much."

Still, it was nice to see that Jasper had decided to make the most of his time with Ella, rather than wasting it sulking.

"Well, is he coming today, or what?" Jasper asked. "Because we're supposed to leave in five minutes."

"Everyone else is here," Ella said, peering down the bus. "Aren't you worried?"

"He'll be here," I said with total confidence. Because he would be. It might have been late when we finally said goodbye, on the corner of my street, but Mac wouldn't miss the competition for the world.

Which wasn't to say he wouldn't cut it a bit fine.

"Everyone here, Miss Anderson?" Mr Carroll leaned against the first row of seats, calling to where Miss Anderson stood, mid-aisle, counting us all.

"Just waiting on one," she called back.

"Let me guess," he said. "Will Macintyre."

"He'll be here," Jasper yelled. "He's got five minutes yet!"

Mr Carroll checked his watch. "Fine. But if he's not here at eight by my watch…" He left the threat unfinished.

"He won't really leave without him, will he?" Ella's eyebrows knitted together.

"Miss Anderson won't let him," Jasper said. "We need him."

"He'll be here," I repeated, still confident.

Letting my head loll to look out of the window, I stared at the gates, smiling at the sight of the wall where Mac had kissed me on the last day of term before Christmas. As I watched, a figure came sauntering round the corner, on to the school drive.

"There he is!" Yasmin called, and I thought I heard Mr Carroll click his tongue in disappointment.

"Well, he'd better hurry up," he said, checking his watch again. But Mac, of course, continued at his own leisurely pace. Even when Mr Carroll stood up and motioned for him to hurry through the window of the minibus, Mac just waved back.

I didn't bother trying to hide my grin.

Mac, I'd decided, was the one thing in my life I wasn't going to worry about. I was going to take a leaf from Jasper's book and just enjoy being with him.

At last, Mac swung himself up on to the bus, skipping the steps entirely, and ignored Mr Carroll as he made his way towards the back of the bus. Towards me.

"Everybody ready for this?" he asked, as Mr Carroll started the engine.

"As we'll ever be," Jasper said.

Mac grinned at Jasper, then dropped into the seat beside me, his arm instantly round my shoulders.

And at that moment, I didn't even care about winning the competition. All I cared about was Mac.

The Schools' Bake-Off competition was being held in central London, about an hour's drive from school.

There had been details on the form, but since I knew Mum had no interest in attending, and I would be going with the rest of the club, I didn't worry too much about exactly where.

So I wasn't entirely prepared for the size of the place. Or the other competitors.

"Are those actual chef's whites?" Jasper murmured in my ear as we climbed the steps into the hall, past groups of kids carrying boxes of equipment. "And were we supposed to bring stuff too?"

"The venue is providing all the basic equipment we need," Miss Anderson said from behind us. "For the recipes we'll be making, it should be more than sufficient." But she looked nervous as well.

Not as nervous as Yasmin, though, who hopped from one foot to the other. "Are we sure we're in the right place? Isn't there a beginners' competition or something?"

"We're not beginners any more," Grace said, looking around with wide eyes. "We're bakers. And we're here to win."

I think she meant it as some sort of rallying cry. Something to get us all psyched up about what lay ahead. Instead, we all just looked on at the scene in front of us with scared expressions.

The gigantic hall had been split into cooking

stations, not unlike the ones we had in school. Except there were no missing handles here, no mismatched tea towels, no dried-on dough on the surfaces that the cleaner hadn't been able to get off. Everything was gleaming white and stainless steel, shiny and ready for work. I spotted a camera crew making their way between the mini kitchens, and everywhere there were kids around our age, all looking perfectly at home, as if they knew exactly what they were doing.

Unlike us.

"I think our stations are over this way," Miss Anderson said, looking dubiously at the map in her hand. "We've got three between us, and they're all next to each other, ready for the group bakes."

We followed her as she weaved through the crowds, Mr Carroll bringing up the rear behind Ella.

"Ready for this?" Mac whispered in my ear.

I shook my head. "Not even a little bit. You?"

"You should just keep thinking about your birthday cake. Maybe that'll help."

He hadn't answered my question. But then, I never really expected Mac to admit to being nervous.

"What are you smiling at?" Jasper asked, as we finally reached the end of the hall where our stations were.

I shrugged. "It's exciting."

"It's terrifying."

"That too," I admitted. "But we're here now. Time to make the most of it."

We didn't have all that long to set up. By the time we'd each claimed our station, working in our usual pairs, and unloaded our ingredients, the judges were already taking to the stage at the front of the hall. When the lead judge stepped up to the microphone, his voice echoed through the massive sound system, bouncing off every corner and hard surface.

To start with, we had the individual competitions. Two hours to bake and decorate the cake, bread or pastry of our choice. Next would come the challenge round – everyone would be given the same recipe and expected to turn out the best version of the item they could. For that one, at least, we got to work in pairs. Then, finally, was the group round. Each group of between four and eight was required to mass-produce some sort of baked goods. After a sample few were sent off to the judges, the rest were to be shared amongst all us bakers – giving us a chance to taste the competition and take our minds off waiting for the results.

When the judge had finished, we were told we had fifteen minutes before the first round. As everyone dashed around doing their last-minute preparation,

Miss Anderson called us together.

"OK, gang. I know this place is a little intimidating. And I know that some of the kids here seem to have been doing this much longer than you."

"You're not making us feel any better, miss," Yasmin pointed out.

Miss Anderson gave her a sympathetic look. "I know we're asking a lot of you here. But you guys are great at this. You really are. You've come on so much in the last term, and I want you to show that to the judges. We're well prepared, we're well practised … so just get out there and bake!"

And that was all we had time for. As the countdown started, Mac squeezed my hand, just once. And then we were off.

For my cake, I'd chosen the Victoria sandwich we made in the second week of Bake Club. I'd figured if it was good enough for Ella's gran, it would be good enough for the judges. Plus, it was a classic. Fantastic when done well, but easy to do badly. I knew I could do it well. Now I just had to prove it to them.

I didn't have a chance to keep an eye on the others. With only two hours to bake, I needed to focus on my own cake. But still, I was constantly aware of Mac beside me, beating and heating his grandma's gingerbread recipe.

Once the cakes were in the oven, things started to calm down. After all, until they were out, there wasn't much most people could do. I, on the other hand, had buttercream to make and jam to prepare. I'd made my own, hijacking a corner of Grace's kitchen the Saturday before, and just prayed it was as good as I remembered.

"Did you weigh your tins again?" Mac asked, from his side of the ovens.

"Of course." I didn't look up; I was concentrating on my icing sugar.

"Not planning on sandwiching them with cake mix?"

I closed my eyes. "No. I'm using buttercream. Like a sane person."

I didn't mean to snap, but I must have done because Mac drifted off to his side of the kitchen again and started clearing up. I wanted to apologize, but there wasn't time. I needed to make the perfect cake first.

I wanted this so badly. I hadn't even realized just how much this competition meant until we reached the venue. This was my first step. In my head, my future unfolded from this moment. Win the competition. Get the apprenticeship. Bake in Paris. Study at the best schools. Go on to conquer the baking world – my own bakery, cookbooks, TV shows … anything was possible.

And it all started here, with one perfect cake.

My sandwich cakes came out of the oven a beautiful golden brown. With a slightly shaking hand, I spread first the jam, then the cream on to the bottom half, and carefully lowered the other cake on top. This wasn't just a matter of satisfying Ella's gran any more. This mattered. A final dusting of icing sugar on the top and I was done.

The judge called time, a huge klaxon going off in case we hadn't heard, and I stepped back. I'd done all I could, I just had to hope it was enough.

The cakes were taken away, all carefully labelled with our names, to the judging chamber, where the judges would taste and rate and decide, while the challenge session took place. In the meantime, we had an hour off to rest, eat lunch and prepare for the next round.

Which left me one more job.

"Hey," I said, reaching up to touch Mac's arm and get his attention. "I'm sorry about before. For snapping at you. I was—"

"Freaking out?" he finished, the warm tone of his voice taking any edge off his words.

"Yeah. Sorry."

He wrapped an arm round my shoulders, holding me close against him, warm and comforting. "That's OK. I know how your perfectionism gets the better of you."

We watched as the judges left the hall, followed by a trail of stewards carrying cakes.

"How was your gingerbread?" I asked. "I didn't get to see."

He just shook his head. "It looked OK, I think. Not perfectly symmetrical, or anything, like yours…"

"It's a bake-off, not a beauty competition," I told him. "It's what it tastes like that matters."

But even as I said it, we saw two cakes going past from the next group over. One was a tiered cake, decorated with fondant icing to look like a top hat. The other was iced to within an inch of its life with beautiful swirls and swags. I glanced over at the kitchens responsible and saw two students in chef's whites looking on nervously.

"We'd better hope so," Mac said, following my gaze. "Otherwise we're going to be in real trouble."

An hour later, after a sandwich and a sit-down, the ushers came round with baskets for each baking station.

Other kids seemed to be opening theirs so,

tentatively, I lifted the tea towel off the top of the basket. There, nestled on top of a pile of ingredients, was the recipe for the challenge round: lemon pie.

Something inside my chest relaxed a little. We could do this. Not just me, all of us. We'd practised pies. We knew pastry, knew blind baking, knew how to test fillings. This was one recipe we could all do really well.

Looking up, I saw relief in Yasmin and Grace's faces and Jasper was grinning, while Ella laid out the ingredients in order, just the way I'd taught her.

"Lemon pie?" Mac read over my shoulder, his breath warm against my cheek. "Sounds good."

"If we're making it, it will be," I said, putting the recipe down and lifting the first of the ingredients out of the basket, wishing my hands weren't shaking so much.

Mac's response to my show of confidence was a slow, lazy smile as he reached for the wooden spoon.

This time when the klaxon went off, Mac and I worked together and it felt much more natural. We'd baked as a pair so often now, we could use each other's strengths and quirks. I knew that Mac was happy to roll out the pastry, but hated trying to get the filling even. He understood that I was obsessive about baking blind, and needed to watch at the oven door constantly until the timer went off.

It worked for us. When the judges called time, we had a flawless lemon pie sitting on the counter, labelled with our names, ready to be tasted and tested.

"It looks perfect," Miss Anderson told us as the ushers carried it away. But that didn't stop the nerves jangling in my belly. Not even Mac's hand gripping mine, a little too tight, did that.

We got another short break then, which gave us time to plan our group bake, even though we'd already been over it a thousand times already. We'd chosen the special cupcakes we'd made for the play, as we knew they were a crowd pleaser, and with their pretty decorations they looked the part. Mac thought they were too girly, but we'd overruled him.

We recreated the set-up we'd had in the Bake Club kitchen, made easier with Mac and Grace on hand this time to help. Mac and I baked half the cakes, Jasper and Ella the other half, with Yasmin and Grace taking on the decoration. We needed to make forty-eight of them in two hours, which was a challenge, but I supposed that was the point. The only way to get them done was to work together.

Barring Yasmin's slight hiccup with the piping bag, everything went well, and two hours later we had our trays of delicately sparkling fairy cupcakes. With shaky hands I packed the best four into a cake box for the judges and then Jasper and Mac laid the rest out on our counters for anyone else who wanted to try. And then, to try and take our minds off what the judges might be saying, we set about tasting every other bake in the room.

"Have you tried the chocolate chip cookies over at kitchen four?" Jasper asked, as he and Ella passed us, cheese straws in hand.

I nodded nervously – they'd been delicious. But Mac said, "They weren't as good as Lottie's," and I couldn't help but smile.

Whatever Mac said, the other cakes and biscuits were amazing. But I had faith in our fairy cupcakes.

Cakes all gone, we had another wait for the final results. The hall was too warm now, too full of different scents, and all the sugar in the air was starting to give me a headache.

"How do you think we did?" Grace asked Miss Anderson, as we all loitered round our baking stations.

Miss Anderson sucked in a breath. "Hard to tell. The standard was very high. But … I think we're in with a chance."

I hoped so. What would happen if we lost? It hadn't

even occurred to me before. My vision of a perfect future had kind of taken over my brain. I'd always known that we probably wouldn't win, but I hadn't thought about the alternative – about what would happen if we totally crashed and burned. Would Bake Club even continue? Or would we all drift away, disillusioned? Winning wasn't everything, of course it wasn't. But without the prospect of possibly winning … would we bother?

I suppose there was still the apprenticeship and Paris. But would Julien even want a bunch of losers competing for a place at his bakery? Maybe he'd just call the whole thing off...

"Stop fretting." Mac was suddenly very close. The heat of his body just behind mine calmed me down. "Nothing we can do about it now, anyway. Think about birthday cake."

Beside me, Jasper, who'd obviously overheard, stifled a laugh. "I don't want to know what that's code for..."

But then, before I could even elbow him in the ribs, the judges were back on stage.

Mac grabbed my hand and I squeezed it back.

This was it.

They read out the results of the individual contest in reverse order, with none of our group placing second or third in the first round. My fingers tightened round Mac's again.

"And in first place," the judge said, and then waited. I held my breath and counted the seconds. "The winner of the individual round is ... Jessica Phillips from Huntingford Girls' School."

Not us.

Not me.

My heart felt like it had seized up. Now what?

The chatter around us quietened as Miss Anderson said, "Still two rounds to go." But if we wanted to win overall, we'd need to do really well in both. And if none of us had even placed in the first round, what were the chances of that?

"For the second, challenge round," the judge said, and we all shut up to listen again. And again, the third and second places went to other schools. Mac's arm crept round my waist, holding me close to him, and I couldn't even say if he was the only thing holding me up. I couldn't do this. I didn't want to listen any more.

"And in first place..." That pause again. That deathly, horrible, gut-eating pause. "Lottie Hansen and Will Macintyre, from St Mary's—" I didn't hear the rest. I was drowning in bodies, with all of Bake Club rushing over and hugging us. I thought Miss

Anderson might be crying. A little aside from the rest of us, even Mr Carroll was smiling.

Then Mac peeled Jasper and Ella off me, wrapped his arms round me and lifted me up on to my tiptoes. "We did it," he whispered in my ear, and my grin grew even wider. We had done it. Together. And I realized, I'd much rather win the pairs comp with Mac than the individual one alone. This ... this was what I'd joined Bake Club for, even if I hadn't known it at the time.

I pulled back a little and smiled up at him. And then I lifted my lips to his and kissed him, soft and sweet. This was our moment, just ours.

Behind us, Mr Carroll said, "That's quite enough of that, thank you," and I realized, a little late, what I'd just done.

It didn't matter right then, anyway. There was still one lot of results for us to hear – the group results. Would we place? Would that be enough?

We quietened down as the judge started to speak again.

"And in our final, third, group round, the results are as follows…"

SCONE PIZZA

1. Heat the oven to 220°C/fan 200°C/gas 7.
2. Mix 250g of plain flour, 1 tsp of salt and 2 tsp of baking powder in a bowl, then rub in 50g of butter.
3. Mix 2 eggs with 3 tbsp of milk, then stir into the dry ingredients to make the dough.
4. Tip out on to a floured surface and shape into a round about 25cm across.
5. Place on a non-stick baking tray, then press out to a circle to make your pizza base.
6. Top with tomato sauce, cheese and whatever else you fancy, then bake for 15 minutes.

The bus home was crazily loud. We'd placed third in the group round – good enough for us to scrape into second place overall. Not a win, but so much better than we could have imagined when we started Bake Club. Grace and Yasmin were trying to start a sing-song, Jasper was reciting bad limericks to Ella, and Mac … Mac sat beside me, smiling contentedly out of the window, as if all his worries were over.

"My parents are away again this weekend, so … victory party at mine tonight?" Grace asked, not loud enough for Mr Carroll to hear at the front of the bus, but loud enough to get an enthusiastic chorus of agreement from the others.

"You going?" Mac asked me.

I deserved to, really. I might never have been invited to one of these things before, but this time, I was part of the reason for the party. And it wasn't like Mum would notice if I wasn't at home.

"Yeah, I think so," I said, and Mac smiled.

"Good."

We barely bothered unloading our stuff into the food tech classroom before we were all racing out of the school grounds, ready to celebrate. It was Saturday and already early evening, but Grace had made a few calls from the bus and it looked like her house would be packed with people again. It was kind of a shame; it would have been nice to celebrate, just us. But apparently Grace wanted to build on the success of her birthday by hosting a mega party. Sure-fire way to boost popularity, I supposed.

In fact, we only just beat the first guests there. Soon the music was up loud, some of the guys from the sixth form arrived with beer, and there were two girls I'd never met before dancing together in the lounge, while the boys cheered them on. I lost Mac for a while, after seeing him wandering out into the garden with some guys I recognized as his friends from school.

I wondered where Grace's parents were. This was the second huge party she'd thrown in, what, a few months? And they were never around at weekends when we baked. I asked Jasper, who shrugged.

"I think they've got a flat in London, closer to the office, and they stay there a lot. Guess they won't be back until next week. Plenty of time to clear up."

The music shifted abruptly and Jasper jumped up. "I love this song! Ella!"

I headed back towards the kitchen, where it was a little quieter. At the counter, two guys were pouring vodka into pint glasses and I realized that while there was plenty of alcohol, no one had brought any food. We hadn't eaten since the group round at the competition, so I was starving. And apparently I wasn't the only one.

"Hey, you." Wandering in from the garden, Mac pressed a kiss to the top of my head. "Is there any food in here?"

I glanced round, searching for our hostess. No sign. "Think Grace will mind if we look?"

Mac was already at the fridge. "Cheese, butter, milk... that's about it."

I yanked open a few cupboard doors. Pasta sauce, but no pasta. Tins of soup. And the baking ingredients we'd left over from Bake Club practice.

Huh. Maybe Grace's parents really weren't here much.

"Is there food?" Jasper asked, appearing at the counter. "I'm starved."

"Not what I'd call food," Mac grumbled. "Maybe we could call for pizza?"

"No need." I grabbed the flour. "Pass me the stuff

from the fridge. I can make you one faster than they could deliver."

"Really?" Jasper asked. "Doesn't the dough need to rise or something?"

I beamed at him. "And to think that five months ago you thought cake mix was the same as buttercream. Now look at you."

Mac dumped the butter and cheese on the counter. "He does have a point though, right?"

I shook my head. "I'll make us a scone pizza. Super easy, quick and yummy."

Jasper gazed around the suddenly crowded kitchen. "You might need to make more than one…"

In the end, I had enough ingredients for five pizzas. Mac watched me make the first pizza base, then took over the mixing.

"Not sure I wanna eat anything you made, man," one of his friends said.

But Mac just raised an eyebrow. "Wait until you taste them."

And they did. Before long, the kitchen was filled with hungry partygoers waiting for the oven timer to go off. Jasper grabbed two slices from the first pizza and ran off to find Ella, while Mac and I ate our own slices before making the next pizza.

As I put the last one in the oven and set the timer

again, Mac tugged on my arm. "Come on."

I followed him into the hallway, almost crashing into him when he stopped abruptly at the bottom of the stairs, pulling me back into the shadows. It reminded me of that first baking session at Grace's, when I'd thought he might kiss me in that exact spot. At first, I thought he'd stopped to avoid the couple coming down the stairs, looking kind of dazed and mussed up. But then, across the way, Ella and Jasper dashed out of the study towards the stairs.

As we watched, Jasper turned to her at the bottom step. "I'm not … this isn't…" He took a breath and started again. "I don't want you to think I'm expecting … anything. You know what I mean? I just want us to make the most of our time together."

Ella nodded. "I know. Me too. Come on," she said, and started up the stairs.

We waited until we were sure they'd gone before we came out of our hiding place.

Mac shook his head. "That's not going to end well."

"How can you be sure?" I asked.

"Long-distance things never do." He gave me a half-smile. "Not our problem, though. Come on. Let's go outside."

The garden was cool, but quieter. We moved

away from the kitchen windows, where I could still hear the clamour as people polished off my pizza. "This way."

Grabbing my hand, Mac pulled me towards the end of the garden. Where the hell were we going? But then, just as I was about to ask, I spotted the trampoline.

"Wanna jump?" Mac asked, waggling his eyebrows at me. "Or are you too sensible for that?"

I glanced behind me; I could still see the kitchen windows. Anyone could be watching.

"Too full of pizza," I said, but I jumped up to sit on the edge of the trampoline, anyway.

Mac boosted himself up beside me, lying flat on the surface of the trampoline, legs dangling off the edge. I smiled at him and he wrapped his arms round my waist, pulling me down to rest my head against his chest.

"Do you think we'll end well?" I asked eventually, after long moments of just feeling his chest rise and fall. I regretted it the moment the words were out, but I couldn't shake the memory of what he'd said about Jasper and Ella.

Shifting to hold me closer and tilting my head up towards his, Mac said, "I don't want to think about this ending at all." Then he lowered his lips to mine.

I knew there were things we should talk about. The apprenticeship, the lies between us. There were so many questions I'd never asked him; but then, he'd never offered up any answers. He wasn't the sort to want to talk about the future, or about his past. And I didn't want him to ask any questions of me, either. And so we lived in this strange always-present, with no past between us, save Mac's weird recollections of me through the years, and no future to worry about past the next bake.

One day, I knew, these things would come back and bite us. All the truths I was avoiding.

But the lies were so much safer.

My hands crept up his back, feeling the smooth lines of his muscles through his shirt. I'd never been this close to anyone before. Never felt this weird mix of emotions – excitement, fear, desire and panic, all at the same time. I wanted Mac to be a part of my life, and right then, he was all mine. He'd chosen me over the party, over his friends. He hadn't taken me upstairs to the bedrooms, like some guys would, like a prize to win. He'd brought me out here, where we could be alone, staring up at the stars, rather than on someone's parents' double bed.

He just wanted to be with me. And that felt incredibly powerful.

His kisses strayed from my lips across my cheek, until he was just resting his lips against my hair, holding me. If I was ever going to tell him my secrets, this was my chance. This moment, right now, was when we should share everything. And I wanted to. There were so many things I wanted to ask him, about his life, his family, his hopes, his dreams. But how could I ask for his secrets when I was still too scared to give him mine?

I could trust Mac, I felt sure of that now. But admitting I'd been lying to him for months... How would he react? I just didn't know. And I wasn't sure I was brave enough to take the risk of finding out.

Suddenly, the truths I couldn't tell were the least of my concerns. Headlights flashed round the side of the house, lighting up our hiding place for a moment. Mac pushed himself up on one elbow, peering into the darkness. Then we heard voices, followed by shouting.

"Grace's parents," I whispered.

Mac nodded. "We need to leave. Now."

Jumping off the trampoline, he grabbed my hand and helped me down. We headed for the side of the house, rather than the kitchen door we'd left by.

My school bag and coat were by the front door where, even now, I could hear Grace's mum shrieking at her daughter and at the strangers in her house. I'd have to collect them later. No way in hell was I going back in there now.

"You've betrayed our trust!" Grace's dad yelled. Around us, kids were streaming out of the house, abandoning the sinking ship.

"If you were ever here, you'd have noticed before now!" Grace shouted back, sounding more upset than angry. "How can I betray you when I never see you?"

For a moment, I paused on the driveway. Grace needed us right now. We should stay. Help.

But if word got back to the school and if Grace's parents complained, told them we had been drinking … The last thing I needed was to give Mr Carroll or Mrs Tyler another reason to visit my mum.

"Stay or go?" Mac asked.

I turned away. "Go."

I made Mac leave me at the corner of Orchard Avenue, sneaking a swift kiss before I headed the rest of the way home alone.

"I'm starting to think you really are ashamed of me," Mac said, holding on to my waist to keep me close.

I gave him an apologetic smile. "It's not that. Really it's not. It's just…"

"You don't want to get into trouble for being seen with me," Mac guessed. "I get it. I'm not the kind of guy you take home."

"No! That's not it." How could he think that? I'd let him kiss me right in front of Mr Carroll. What more could I do?

"Then what is it? At the competition today, you didn't seem to mind." The confusion and hurt on his face made my heart ache. "Is it your mum? Is she overprotective or something?"

Quite the opposite. "No."

"Then let me walk you home."

I paused, a moment too long.

"What's going on, Lottie?" Mac asked, and I wanted to tell him, so badly. But how could I? After we'd been so close the last couple of days, how could I tell him I'd been lying to him all along?

"I'm sorry," I said, slipping out of his grasp. "I'll see you at school on Monday."

I didn't let myself cry as I unlocked the door and went into the house. Not even when the tower of takeaway containers on the hall table finally lost its balance and crashed down on top of me. In fact, I didn't cry at all until I got to my room, barely responding to Mum's call to check it really was me.

But then I threw myself on my bed and sobbed.

Maybe it was the emotion of the day. The competition, the fear, the exhilaration. Maybe it was Mac thinking I was ashamed of him, like I supposed his father was. When the only thing I was ashamed of was myself. My life. My lies.

God, I hated lying to him. I wanted, more than anything, to tell him the truth. But how could I? How could I expect him to forgive me for all the lies?

And even if he did, who'd want to be with a girl whose whole life was as messed up as mine? Who'd even want to be that girl's friend?

If Mac knew, he'd want me to tell the others. Jasper. Ella. Yasmin. Grace.

Grace. I wondered if she was OK. Yeah, she wasn't exactly my best friend, but she was a member of Bake Club. And it was a Bake Club party. Mac and I should have stayed with the rest of them to face the consequences. And instead I'd run, because I was so damn scared of all my lies coming crashing down.

What kind of friend did that make me?

PECAN LOAF

1. Heat the oven to 180°C/fan 160°C/gas 4.
2. Mix together 300g of plain flour, 150g soft brown sugar, 1 tbsp of baking powder, ½ tsp salt and 75g of chopped pecan nuts.
3. In another bowl, whisk together 250ml of milk, 75ml of maple syrup, ½ tsp vanilla extract, 2 eggs and 20g of melted and cooled butter.
4. Add the wet ingredients to the dry and stir to combine.
5. Pour the mixture into a greased and lined 900g loaf tin and bake for 45 to 50 minutes, or until a cake tester comes out clean.

"I'm just saying, we need somewhere to practise." Jasper shifted uncomfortably on the leather seats outside Mr Carroll's office. I wondered if *he'd* ever been called here. Right now, he was just bugging me while I waited for the Head of Year to call me in. Again.

"I know we do," I replied, staring at the posters above Jasper's head. One about striving for excellence. One about working together. None about dealing with possible boyfriends who made you cake but thought you were ashamed of them. "Any bright ideas?"

Jasper ticked off the options on his hands. "Well, Grace's is out. Obviously. Food tech classrooms? Maybe Miss Anderson could get us some extra hours?"

I shook my head. "She already tried. Carroll says we need to be studying for our exams, not taking on more after-school activities." And then he'd called me to his office again. I wasn't entirely convinced the two events weren't linked.

"Well, mine's no good," Jasper said. "My parents see patients at the house on weekends. Besides, they don't cook. I couldn't even swear we've got mixing bowls."

I looked at him, curious. "What do you eat?"

"Takeaways, mostly. You know, you can get food from pretty much anywhere in the world delivered. We had North African last night."

Weird. Just when I thought I knew how odd Jasper was, I found a whole new level.

"What'll it be tonight, then?"

Jasper's face fell, his gaze sliding away to the floor. "Italian, I think. Ella's mum's in town again, wants to go out."

"Ella invited you too?" That was good, right? After Grace's party, they'd seemed closer again. Maybe Ella was going to tell her mum she wanted to stay.

"Her mum did." Jasper didn't look very enthusiastic about it. "I'm not sure it'll make any difference, though."

I wanted to ask more – about that night at Grace's and what had really happened between them. But then Mr Carroll's door opened. He scowled at Jasper, then turned to me. "Come on in, Lottie."

Mr Carroll's office hadn't got any more friendly since the last time I was in there. And apparently, his opinion of me hadn't changed much, either. I was still on the wrong track.

He folded his hands on the desk and asked, "How are your sessions with Mrs Tyler going, Lottie?"

I shrugged. "OK, I guess." I lied to her about my life, she wrote notes, everyone's happy. Wasn't that how these things were supposed to work?

"She's expressed some concerns about you," he said, staring at me, waiting for a reaction. "And I have to admit, I agree with her assessment."

"I'm fine," I said, emphasis firm on both words. "I'm taking part, my grades are up … I did everything you wanted."

"Yes, well … it's the taking part that's the problem." He sat back in his chair. "Do you want to tell me what happened at Grace Stewart's house last Saturday night?"

Ah. So that was what this was about. "I heard there was a party."

"You heard?"

"Yeah." Her parents hadn't seen me. Maybe no one would have mentioned my presence.

"I have heard, from several people, that not only were you there, but you actually baked for the event."

Oh well, no point denying it now. "Everyone loves pizza."

Mr Carroll sighed. "When I asked you to start taking part in school events, these weren't the ones I was hoping you'd choose."

"But it's my choice, right? I joined Bake Club, did work experience, made friends, catered for the school play… I helped us come second in a national competition…"

"You started dating Will Macintyre."

I looked away, aware I was blushing. "My friends, relationships, whatever. They're none of the school's business."

"They are if we believe they're affecting your well-being," Mr Carroll countered. "That boy is a bad influence. Mrs Tyler is concerned that, during this vulnerable time, he could damage your chances of doing well in your exams."

The exams. Of course they were all that mattered. It made no difference to them that Mac made me happy.

"Look," he said, trying one last-ditch attempt at the friendly approach. "Mrs Tyler wants to talk with your mother. In fact, she wants us all to sit down together, at school or at your house, if that's more comfortable for everyone…"

"No!" I sat bolt upright in my chair, my heart pounding so loudly I could barely hear myself over it.

"It's important, Lottie. This is your future at stake."

"I'll stay away from Mac, then," I found myself saying. "I'll do whatever you want. Just don't call my mum." Mr Carroll stared at me, apparently surprised by my outburst. "She's had enough to deal with," I finished lamely. "I don't want to worry her."

"Mrs Tyler is already trying to set up a visit," he said. Then his face softened, just a little, and I knew I'd won. "I'll have a word with her. But if we think it's necessary…"

"Got it." I grabbed my bag from the floor beside my chair. "Is that it?"

Mr Carroll nodded and I ran for it, Jasper chasing me down the corridor and the stairs as I went.

"What did he say?" Jasper asked, slightly out of breath, as we reached the fresh air and safety of the playground.

"Just the usual. The importance of studying over baking. I pointed out we still don't have anywhere *to* bake." A lie, but it got us back on to the subject at hand. "We really do need to do something about that."

Jasper wasn't looking at me, though. He was

looking up at the office window, directly above us. And when I followed his gaze, I saw Mr Carroll, watching us through the glass.

"He really called you up there just for that?" Jasper asked.

"What can I say? He's obsessed."

"Lottie." Mac's voice, directly behind me, made my heartbeat skip. His hand, circling my waist, sent me into a blind panic.

I spun round to face him, pulling away as I did so. Out of his reach, out of his life. Out of anything Mr Carroll could call trouble. "Hi. We were just talking about finding somewhere to bake. In fact, we just need to—"

"What's wrong?" Mac's forehead crumpled into a confused frown. "What's happened?"

"Nothing. Just busy." I smiled brightly. "Actually, Jasper and I really do need to get going."

"No, we don't," Jasper said, looking at me like I'd lost my mind. Which I was starting to think I had, picking him for a best friend. Couldn't he play along with a simple lie?

"Don't worry, Jasper," Mac said, his face stormy. "I get it."

"Well, I don't!" Jasper turned to me. "Is this something to do with Mr Carroll?"

"You've been in to see Carroll?" Mac asked. "What did he say?"

I glared at Jasper, but I could feel my hands starting to shake. "I told you. That was just about Bake Club. And we're supposed to be meeting Yasmin at food tech right now. Come on." I grabbed Jasper's arm, and started pulling him in the right direction. He resisted for a moment, but finally gave in.

I couldn't help one final glance up at Mr Carroll's window, though. He was still watching. And as I turned back towards food tech, I realized Mac had seen him too. He scowled up at the window, fists clenched at his sides.

He looked furious.

I dragged Jasper all the way to the food tech classroom, ignoring his questions. Apart from anything else, if I thought too hard about what I'd just done, I'd probably cry. Mac didn't follow us, thankfully, but Ella, Grace and Yasmin were already there anyway, talking about our lack of options.

"Well, since we obviously can't practise at Grace's house any more," Yasmin said, with an apologetic nod at Grace, "we need to come up with somewhere else if we want to bake our best for Julien."

"For Paris," Grace added, and I just knew she

was thinking about French boys and shopping, not baking.

"That's what I said," Jasper agreed. "Lottie said Miss Anderson couldn't get us any more hours here, so it'll have to be one of our houses."

Eyes started to turn towards me – I knew exactly where this was going. And I couldn't let it. Not when I'd just ruined everything with Mac to protect this secret. "She only said we couldn't have extra time after school," I said. "But I bet she'd let us practise at lunchtime and maybe even before school when she's getting set up. I mean, we're here anyway. And that would give us more time than if we were at anyone's house."

Murmurs of agreement, the odd nod … and I started to feel myself relax again, for the first time that day.

Lucky for me, Miss Anderson agreed with my idea. She was always at school by seven forty-five, anyway, and she said she'd appreciate the company. I was pretty sure that last part wasn't completely true, but I didn't call her on it.

The one thing I'd forgotten, of course, was that Mac had to work at the garage before school. Still, everyone else made it most days, getting in a quick batch of cakes before classes, or practising our decorating skills. Mac joined us at lunchtime and him being busy actually made life easier.

Things were a little awkward between us after the scene outside Mr Carroll's office, but seeing him in the relative privacy of the food tech classroom meant I could show him I wasn't ashamed of him in front of our friends, at least, and by Thursday we were almost back to normal.

Until my weekly appointment with Mrs Tyler came round.

In my defence, I wasn't expecting to see him there. Every other week I'd managed to slip into the counsellor's office unseen. But this week, as I turned the corner on to Mrs Tyler's corridor, there was Mac, walking towards me.

"Hey," he said, grinning. "You on your way to class?"

I tried to smile back, but it felt weak, forced. Already I was staring over his shoulder at Mrs Tyler's door, willing her to stay inside. And when Mac reached out to rest his hand at my waist, the way he did every day at Bake Club, it took real effort not to flinch away. The last thing I needed, after my promise to Mr Carroll, was Mrs Tyler seeing me and Mac together.

"Um, sort of," I said. "Just need to do something first."

"Want me to walk you?"

I shook my head, a little too hard. "No, no. I'm fine. Besides, don't you have a lesson of your own to get to?"

"Geography. I don't think they'll miss me too much." He dipped his head, as if he were about to kiss me. "And I've missed you..."

Behind him, Mrs Tyler's door opened.

I pulled away from Mac, so fast that he had to put a hand on the wall to keep his balance.

"What the—?" Mac glanced behind him. "Oh, I get it." When he looked back at me, his eyes were dark. "What are you afraid of, Lottie?" he murmured.

I just shook my head. I couldn't tell him.

Mac's mouth tightened and, before I could even think to stop him, before I even realized what he was doing, he smacked his palm against the wall, sending an echoing crack down the corridor.

Spinning to face Mrs Tyler he moved towards her. She took a step back, her eyes wide, and I dashed forward to try and get between them, my heart racing. But Mac grabbed my arm before I could get past him.

"I don't know what you've said to her, you and

Carroll, but it doesn't matter." Mac's voice was low, and harder than any sixteen year old's should be. "She's with me. We're together. And I don't care if you don't think I'm good enough for her. All that matters is what Lottie thinks."

Oh God. I swallowed and it felt like a rock cake was lodged in my throat. Tiny tremors rippled through my body, making my knees feel like they could give way at any moment.

Mrs Tyler's gaze landed on me. "All I've ever told Lottie is to think about her future," she said, her voice calm and mild. "About what will make her happy. Lottie, do you think that dating this boy will do that?"

What could I say? How could I tell her about birthday cake in a locked school, or stolen moments at a party, when she was millimetres away from paying my mum a visit?

But how could I lie and say that Mac didn't make me happy? It would hurt him. But it might save my family from being torn apart even more...

The lie won.

Mac stared at me, his cheeks getting redder with every moment I hesitated, every second that went by without my answer. And when I slid my gaze from his...

"Right. I get it." Dropping my arm like it burned him, he stalked away down the corridor. I didn't turn to watch him go, but another echoing crack from the next corridor over made my whole body shake.

"Come on," Mrs Tyler said, reaching out to take my arm. I yanked it away, and she sighed. "I've got some tissues inside."

It was only then I realized I was crying.

I ran all the way to Bake Club after a mostly silent hour with Mrs Tyler. All I could think was that I had to talk to Mac, I had to explain. I couldn't tell him the truth or I'd lose him for good, but there had to be some lie, something I could say to make him forgive me.

But when I got there, Yasmin stood in Mac's place at our workstation, and Mac was with Grace, their heads bent over his mixing bowl together.

"What's going on?" Yasmin asked, pulling her ingredients from her basket. "Mac just kicked me out!"

I winced. "Sorry. We had a little ... disagreement." Understatement of the year.

"I kind of guessed that much."

I looked over at the other station again. Grace was giggling as Mac stirred the mixture. A horrible, sick feeling started rising up in my throat. "I need to talk to him. I need to sort this out."

Yasmin stared at me, and whatever she saw in my face, it obviously convinced her I needed help.

"Just get through this bake," she said. "Once we're done, I'll distract Grace during clean-up. You can talk to him then."

I nodded, the movement jerky. How was I supposed to bake when Mac was flirting with Grace just metres away?

In the end, Yasmin did most of the work, while I tried to ignore Jasper and Ella's concerned glances. Eventually, whatever it was we'd made was in the oven, and I could talk to Mac.

"Now?" I asked Yasmin, stripping off my apron and tossing it on to the counter.

Yasmin looked dubiously across at Grace and Mac. "Yeah, OK."

I don't know what she said to Grace and I didn't care. I was too focused on fixing things.

"I'm sorry," I said, before Mac had even looked up and noticed I was there. "I should have ... I didn't mean it. You know I care about you. I really, really do. It's just—"

"Lottie, stop it." He sounded tired, and when I looked at his hands the knuckles were red raw.

"I just wanted to explain."

He laughed; a bitter, horrid sound.

"Look, Lottie. You've made it pretty clear you don't want to be seen with me outside Bake Club. I thought... Well, it doesn't matter. But if I'm not good enough for you outside this room, I'm not going to try and be good enough in it. I baked in your stupid competition because it mattered to you and to the others. And I'll try for this apprenticeship, I guess, because... Well, maybe it might be something. But that's it. I'm not going to try and be someone I'm not to satisfy people I don't care about. And I'm not giving up the rest of my life, and my other choices, for you."

"I'm not asking you to," I said quietly. Because I had no right to ask him for anything. All I'd done was lie to him since we met. To think that I'd believed he would be embarrassed to be seen with me outside Bake Club. And now he thought that I was ashamed of him. "I just... I do care about you, even if you don't believe it. I wish..." I shook my head. We'd gone too far for that now. "I hope you get the future you deserve. I hope you win that apprenticeship and it's the start of something for you."

His smile was cruel. "No, you don't. Because I'd

have to beat you to do it. And you can't let anyone think you're anything less than perfect, can you?"

What could I say to that? He didn't even know how true it was. And I couldn't tell him.

So I did the only thing I could think of to prove him wrong. I waited until the others had gone, and then I went back in to talk to Miss Anderson.

"I don't want to be considered for the apprenticeship."

Miss Anderson looked up from her desk at my blurted-out words. "Come in and sit down, Lottie."

Miserably, I shut the food tech door behind me and headed over to her desk. She was going to try and talk me out of this. But it was the only thing I could think of to try and make things right.

I perched on the edge of the chair nearest her desk. "I know it's presumptuous to assume I'd get picked anyway, but just in case I was hoping you could tell Julien not to consider me. I'll bake, so the others don't think it's weird, but I can't win."

"Why?"

I'd prepared for this one, at least. "I've got too much on this summer. I'll be getting ready to start A levels, I've got plans with Mum. And besides, I like baking, but I'm not sure I'm considering it as a career."

All lies.

Miss Anderson raised her eyebrows at me. "Nothing to do with Mac, then?"

I shook my head. "Not at all. But ... he really does deserve it. He's a great baker and he'd do a great job there."

"So would you," Miss Anderson said and my gut clenched.

"Maybe."

She gave me an intense kind of a look, the sort that said, "Ignore me at your peril!"

"Lottie, listen to me. You can't give up your own hopes and ambitions for anyone, let alone a boy."

"I'm not—" I started, but she held up a hand to stop me.

"Besides which, you can't presume to know what's best for other people, either. Maybe Mac doesn't want this apprenticeship. Honestly, he hasn't seemed all that interested when I've mentioned it."

"But that's just because—" I stopped myself this time. Not my secret to tell. I was trying to make things better with Mac, not worse.

"Because?"

I shook my head. "It doesn't matter. But he is interested, trust me."

"Well, then, he's going to have to show it. And

work for it. Just like everyone else." She gave me a stern look. "Including you."

CHOCOLATE BROWNIES

1. Heat the oven to 180°C/fan 160°C/gas 4.
2. Melt 175g of butter and 175g of dark chocolate together in a large heavy-based saucepan.
3. In a bowl beat together 3 eggs, 250g of caster sugar and 1½ tsp of vanilla extract.
4. Once the chocolate mixture has cooled, beat in the egg and sugar mixture, then add 110g of plain flour and ½ tsp salt.
5. Stir in 100g of white chocolate chips.
6. When it's all combined, pour the mixture into a lined brownie pan.
7. Bake for about 25 minutes, until the top looks dry. The inside should still be gooey and delicious!

But by the next day, Mac winning the apprenticeship wasn't my biggest concern. Because that night, I heard the sirens screeching down the road to the school, almost drowning out my ringtone.

And when I answered the phone, it was Jasper.

"You've got to get down to the police station, now. Mac's been arrested."

Jasper beat me there, but that wasn't surprising.

"What happened?" I asked, racing up the steps to the police station, my lungs tight. I'd run all the way from my house, praying I'd closed the front door quietly enough that Mum didn't notice I'd left. It was gone eleven and I should be in bed, but she wouldn't leave her room to check on me unless she'd heard something. "And how did you know about it before me?" If Mac had called Jasper and not me when this happened, then there really was no hope for us.

But that wasn't the issue right now. *Focus, Lottie.*

"There was a fire at the school," Jasper said. "The

food tech classroom. They caught Mac running away."

No! I didn't believe it. Whatever they thought had happened, there had to be another explanation. "It doesn't make any sense! He loves that place. Why would he burn it down?"

"That's what Miss Anderson said when she called my mum."

"Miss Anderson called your mum? Why?"

"Specialist teen psychologist, remember?" Jasper said. "I guess she thought she might be able to help. I begged to come with her. I knew you'd want to come here and what kind of a friend would I be to leave you here alone? Come on, it's freezing."

It was late, but the police station was still full of people. Tired-looking officers, some boys I vaguely recognized from the sixth form, an older man sitting with his head in his hands. Jasper and I sat on uncomfortable metal chairs, ignoring the looks from everyone who walked past and waited. And while I waited, I tried to make sense of things in my head.

Mac wouldn't burn down the food tech classroom. They were just jumping to conclusions based on his record. He wouldn't hurt Bake Club. Especially this close to the apprenticeship bake-off.

Unless… Was this my fault? He was mad at me, sure. But he'd said he'd still try for the apprenticeship.

What else? What if he'd confronted Mr Carroll? What if Mr Carroll had said something to Mac? Told him to stay away from me? Or banned him from Bake Club? That could do it, maybe, given how angry and frustrated Mac had been lately. It could all be Mr Carroll's fault.

As well as mine.

I pulled my coat more tightly round me as Jasper wrapped an arm over my shoulder. "It'll be OK," he murmured. But I couldn't see how it possibly would be.

An hour later, Mac finally emerged from some interrogation room somewhere, his dad at his side, face grim. I nudged Jasper awake beside me and we leaped to our feet, but they didn't stop for us. Mac's dad was already grabbing his arm, dragging him out of the station.

"Worthless piece of…" his dad muttered as they went past. "Don't know why I bothered coming to get you."

"I didn't ask you to," Mac said. Had he even seen us? I couldn't be sure. We followed anyway. "I wanted Jamie."

"Yeah, well, your brother's as big a waste of space as you. Probably off with some bird somewhere."

"At least Jamie would have asked if I did it,"

Mac said, and I almost stopped walking. We shouldn't be listening to this. Mac wouldn't want us to hear this.

But Jasper's mum had come out with them and we had to follow her, didn't we? And they were talking in a public place...

"You ungrateful..." Mac's dad stopped, turning to face his son, yanking him round so he had to look back. I saw Mac's face tighten and I knew he'd seen us. Knew he hated that we were watching this.

"I didn't have to ask," Mac's dad said, his voice hard. I flinched at the sound of it. "I know. Of course you did it. Once a criminal, always a criminal. You're ungrateful, that's your problem. I've given you a roof over your head and brought you up alone all these years, and this is how you repay me."

Mac had gone very, very still. For a moment, I thought he might hit his dad, but he didn't. Instead, he spoke in a low, tight voice. "Jamie brought me up more than you did. And you only gave us a roof because you wanted us to grow up and run your garage for you, while you got fat and drunk. But I'm your son, not your servant." Mac grabbed his dad's hand and ripped it away from where he held his arm. "And I quit."

He turned and walked out, not looking back at

us, not seeing the way his dad froze and stared after him. It took me a moment to come to my senses, but when I did, I raced after him.

"Mac!" I called, and he turned to look at me. But there was no warmth in his face. There was barely even recognition.

"I-I know you didn't do this."

He didn't smile. "Then you're the only one who does."

"Are you OK?" A stupid question, but I hadn't a clue what else to say.

Mac raised an eyebrow at me. "What do you care? Isn't this just what you thought would happen? Isn't this why I wasn't good enough for you?"

"No!" How could he think that? God, how badly had I screwed this up if that was how he thought I felt about him? "That's not true. I told you, I care about you—"

"Don't lie to me, Lottie." His voice was low, mean, and I knew he was barely keeping a hold on his temper. "You don't have to do that any more."

He turned away before I could tell him that, for once, I was telling the truth.

But I couldn't just let him leave. "Where will you go?"

He didn't bother to turn back to face me. "I've

got places I can stay. You don't need to worry about me." And with that, he walked away.

Jasper's mum came to stand beside me, Jasper hovering behind. I'd almost forgotten she was there. "Come on," she said. "Let's get you home to bed."

The next day was awful. Exhausted from the night before and the nightmares that had interrupted my sleep since I got home, I was late to classes, and once I was there it was impossible to concentrate. The fire, it seemed, had only really affected the food tech classroom, off to one side of the technology building. That block was closed, cordoned off by metal barriers, with the caretaker patrolling it during breaks, but the rest of the school was open for business as usual. Unfortunately.

Bake Club met at lunchtime in the canteen, surrounded by too many other people staring at us, wanting to know what had happened. We ignored them, just like we ignored the fact that Mac wasn't there. Might never be there again. I didn't even know where he was staying, if he'd been expelled, or whether his dad would let him come home. But nobody was talking about that...

"I can't believe this!" Grace's voice grew shrill on the last word. "The Paris bake-off is this weekend!"

"We know, Grace." Jasper sounded as tired and irritable as I felt.

"How could he do this?" Ella asked, sounding more confused than angry. "I thought he liked us."

"He didn't do it," I said firmly. But Jasper's look across the table told me I was the only one who believed it.

"It wouldn't be the first time," Grace pointed out.

"He has been pretty mad lately," Ella added.

"Lottie." Jasper's voice was softer than the others, like he was letting down a small child. "He practically admitted it last night. He said you were the only one who didn't believe it."

I shook my head. "No. He didn't do it."

"This is your fault!" Grace burst out. "If you hadn't driven him crazy by... What the hell did you do to him anyway?"

"It doesn't matter," I muttered.

"It does if it made him burn down my chance at Paris! So what happened? One minute you were all over each other, all the freaking time, the next he was helping me to make pecan loaf and looking miserably at you!"

"Nothing happened," I lied. Why stop now? "And I told you. He didn't do this."

"Why?" Grace asked. "Because you think you

298

changed him? Tamed the bad boy?"

"Because he loved Bake Club." I stared at her. "You all saw that. He wouldn't do this."

"Does it really matter?" Yasmin asked quietly. "I mean, right now? The police will look into it, the school will do whatever they need to do. But right now we have a bake-off on Sunday and we have nowhere to practise."

She had a point. The table fell silent and listened. "Look, Grace's house is still out, Jasper's doesn't have the equipment, Ella's gran couldn't cope with us all at hers, my house is too full of people all the time…" She looked at me and a chill settled over my body. "I think it has to be Lottie's. The renovation on your kitchen must be done by now, right? I'm sure your mum wouldn't mind, just for tonight and tomorrow, would she?"

"We can't practise at mine." The words came out sharply, like broken ice.

"Why not?" Grace's brow crinkled. "Your dad must have had all the stuff, right?"

"It won't work," I said. "Mum has … something on. We can't."

"Well, ask her!" Grace said, exasperated. "We need this, Lottie, and you're the only option. It's what a proper friend would do."

It was, I knew. And I still couldn't do it. "Well, maybe we're not proper friends," I said, hating myself even as I spoke. The bile in my stomach was churning, making me feel sick. "Maybe I only joined the stupid club to get Mr Carroll off my back. I never wanted to be part of it anyway. And now Mac's gone..." I shook my head. "I don't even want to win the stupid apprenticeship."

They stared at me, shades of horror, amazement and shock on their faces. My teeth clamped down on the inside of my cheek to keep from crying, the pain a distraction from the acid rising up in my throat.

Pushing my chair back, I got to my feet, grabbed my bag and walked out. I heard Jasper calling behind me, but I didn't stop. I couldn't stop.

I wasn't part of Bake Club any more.

I was just me. Alone.

The worst part was, I still had to make it through afternoon lessons. God knows I didn't want to. I thought about running home, slamming my bedroom door and hiding in there forever, just like my mum, with the covers over my head. But what was the point of letting down my friends, Mac, Miss Anderson, myself, if it didn't keep the school from finding out about Mum? And if I skipped a whole afternoon's lessons, you could bet they would call. So instead I sat in my classes, learned absolutely nothing and tried to avoid the stares and whispers from the other students. In fact, the only ones not whispering and staring were the Bake Club guys.

Thankfully, I didn't have classes with any of them that afternoon, but I caught a glimpse of Jasper jogging towards me across the yard until Ella pulled him back. At least someone realized I wanted to be alone.

The moment the bell rang, I was out of there, racing down the drive to the school gates. Home, crazy as it was, was the place you went when everything else went to hell, right? When it was the only place you had left.

But when I got there, it turned out I might as well not have bothered with the afternoon at all.

"Your school called." Mum spoke the moment I walked through the door into the maze of Stuff, and it took me a moment to realize she was actually there. Not hiding upstairs, waiting for me to find her. There. Talking to me.

I let the door go behind me. "They did?"

Mum nodded. "They want to talk to me. They want to visit. What's going on, Lottie? What's happened?"

"I don't know. Maybe it's just GCSE stuff. Or course options for sixth form." When in doubt, lie.

"Why would they need to come here?" Mum looked around her, her eyes widening, as if she were seeing the Stuff for the first time. "They can't come here!"

I threw my bag to the floor and it sent a cascade of magazines falling with it. "Don't you think I know that!" The bile and the sick feeling that had stayed with me all afternoon had gone now. I was done feeling guilty, feeling sorry, feeling responsible. And all that was left was my anger. "Don't you think I've done everything I can to stop them! I've given up everything to try and keep people away from this ... pit! I've lost my friends, I've disappointed my teachers, I even... God, I even let Mac go and look what happened then! I've tried, Mum. I've done everything I can. But they're coming anyway. And everyone is going to find out!" Tears, hot and furious, fell on my cheeks and as I brought up my hands to wipe them away, I heard a familiar voice from behind me.

"Sweet Jesus..." Jasper whispered.

I spun round, shame burning in my cheeks as I saw him standing on the doorstep, staring in, Ella, Yasmin and Grace behind him. I couldn't tell which hurt more. The pity or the horror in their eyes. I glanced back. Mum had already gone, back to her nest, no doubt. Ashamed, maybe, for the first time. And leaving me to deal with everything.

"What are you doing here! How did you get in?" I stepped forward and tried to slam the door, but a rogue takeaway carton that had landed on the frame stopped it from shutting properly.

"We came to see if you were all right," Ella said and another tear burned my cheek.

I kicked the takeaway carton out of the way. "I don't need your help," I hissed, and slammed the door in their faces.

And then I slid down to sit on the landslide of magazines and sobbed.

I didn't eat dinner that night, or breakfast the next morning. Didn't answer Mum's knock on my bedroom door. Or the eight phone calls from Jasper. I ignored the entire world for as long as I could. Until, on Saturday evening, it came knocking on my bedroom window.

At the first knock, I pulled the duvet over my head.

"I'm not going away." The words were muffled through the glass, but I still recognized the voice. Mac. Not him too. What had they told him?

"I brought brownies," he added. My stomach rumbled. "Chocolate brownies. With chocolate chips. Home-made."

I was starving. I was sad and lonely and hungry, and I wanted to talk to Mac. But how could I, after all the lies I'd told?

"Lottie." I heard his sigh, even through the glass. "I'm staying here until you talk to me."

And he would. Mac was stubborn. Maybe even as stubborn as me. Plus he had brownies on his side.

I squeezed my eyes tight to get the last of the tears out, wiped my face on my pillow, then crawled out from under my duvet. I looked a sight, but it didn't matter any more.

Mac smiled as I appeared at the window and backed up across the garage roof as I opened it to let him in. He was almost too big to fit, his shoulders too wide, but he climbed through and landed with a lot more grace than I would have managed.

"What do you want?" I asked, dropping back to sit on my bed and holding my hand out for a brownie.

Mac glanced round the room, then chose my desk chair as his seat. "Nice room," he said, opening the tin and handing me cake. "Spartan."

"You mean empty." My own, clean, empty haven, away from the rest of the house. Not that it mattered now. "What do you want?" I asked again.

He looked down at his hands, folded in his lap. He was wearing jeans and a jumper, his hair messy. And when he looked up, I noticed the bruising round his eye. Jamie again? Or his dad this time? Had he even gone home yet?

"I wanted to tell you about the fire," he said, and my gaze jerked to his in surprise.

"This one or the last one?" Because, really, if we were letting out the truth at last, we might as well get all of the secrets out of the way.

"This one, for now," Mac said. "If you want, I'll tell you about the other later."

I nodded. One truth at a time, I supposed. "Go on, then. What happened?"

Mac sighed. "It was the pecan loaf."

"The one you're practising for Julien?"

"Yeah. I couldn't do it at home. Too time-consuming – Dad would notice."

"So you broke into the school?"

He nodded. "I wanted to see what it would taste like if I toasted the pecans first. But while I had them toasting, I heard someone coming and had to get out quickly."

All this, just because his dad was too stupid to let him bake at home.

"And you didn't have time to turn the hob off," I guessed. Things were starting to come together in my head. "I told everyone you didn't do it. That you wouldn't."

"Not intentionally," Mac agreed. "I tried to get back in, later, to turn it off. But it was too late. That's why I was still there when the police and the fire brigade were called."

"How you got caught."

"Yeah."

"Have you been home yet?"

Mac shrugged. "Where else would I go?"

I didn't point out that he'd said he had places to stay. I should have known that was just his pride talking. "What did your dad say?"

Mac tilted his head so I could get a better look at his black eye. "A man of few words."

"Bastard." Utter, utter bastard.

"Yeah. But maybe I deserved it this time. I've really screwed things up." He looked so miserable at the thought, I scooted closer to the desk, reaching out across the gap between us to hold his hand.

"You never deserve that," I told him. "Still. What happens now?"

Mac squeezed my fingers. "We wait and see. I've explained everything to Miss Anderson. Told her about Dad, the whole lot. She's talking to the Head for me, and the police. Jasper's mum too."

"That's good. You've got people on your side."

"So have you, you know."

"Other than you?" I shook my head. "I don't think so. Not any more."

Mac tilted his head to smile at me. "Who do you think called me?"

I looked up. "Jasper?" Maybe Jasper didn't hate me.

"First, yeah. Then Ella. Then Yasmin. Then even Grace. They all told me I had to come and talk to you, make you see sense. Make you come back to Bake Club."

A warm, happy bubble started to form in my chest. "They still want me?"

"Of course they do." He shifted, coming to sit beside me on the bed. "Not as much as me, but yeah. They want you."

I tucked my head against his shoulder, solid and comforting under my cheek. Mac kissed my hair and, just for a moment, everything felt OK again.

Until Mac said, "But we also want to know why you lied to us."

It was only fair, I knew that. He'd told me his truth, now I had to tell mine. But where did it start? "Give me another brownie then."

Mac chuckled, but reached for the tin. It was the same battered old biscuit tin he'd brought me my birthday cake in.

I considered, as I chewed. "I guess I didn't know what else to do. When it started – Mum's hoarding, I mean – I didn't really have anyone to tell. After Dad died, I blocked everyone off. And then Mr Carroll called me into his office. Told me I needed to make an effort to take part, to be involved in school activities, or they'd have to talk to my mum. And I couldn't let that happen. So I joined Bake Club."

"Jasper said you told them you only joined because of Mr Carroll," Mac said, like he hadn't believed it at the time.

"I did," I admitted. I looked up at him, hoping he could see some other truths in my face. "But that's not why I stayed."

Mac smiled, bent forward, and kissed me lightly. "Brownie crumbs," he said. "So, what happened next?"

"I stayed," I said. "I made friends. I … saw Mrs Tyler, the school counsellor, once a week, and lied to her about things at home. And then she started getting concerned about me spending time with you."

"So I wasn't imagining the part where you were ashamed of me."

"Not ashamed," I said, fast. "Never that. I just…

I was scared if they knew how much you meant to me, they'd make a big thing about it. Call Mum."

Mac's eyes were dark. "How much do I mean to you?"

I swallowed. I owed him this. But it was so hard to find the words. "You brought me brownies when all I've done is lie to you for months."

"I think that says more about what you mean to me."

I looked away. "I told Miss Anderson you should get the apprenticeship. Told her I don't want to be considered."

Mac went still. "You shouldn't have done that."

"You need it more."

"I can't take it, even if they offer it to me."

"You should."

We were silent for a moment, the quiet stretching out between us. "It doesn't matter now, anyway," Mac said finally. "Julien won't want a known arsonist in his bakery."

"You were always that," I pointed out. "It was the first thing I ever knew about you."

"And what do you know about me now?" Mac asked.

"That I want to be with you." My breath caught

in my throat as I spoke the words. "And I don't care who knows it."

Mac shook his head. "That's not all you know."

"No?"

"No." He leaned forward and kissed me again, long and sweet. "You know that I want to be with you too."

And I did. He'd shown me, through cake, through every moment we spent together and every lie he never told me – even when he told them to everyone else. Will Macintyre wanted to be with me – just me. And I felt like the luckiest girl in the world.

"I'm sorry," I said, even though it was far too late, really, "about everything. With Mr Carroll, and Mrs Tyler."

Mac let out a breath. "I just wish you'd told me the truth. Trusted me to help."

"I couldn't." I swallowed, feeling tears burning again at the back of my eyes. "I wanted to, so much. But I was scared you'd hate me for lying to you. And I was so scared about the school finding out. I couldn't risk them taking me away from Mum. I'm all she has." A sob escaped my throat. "I'm so sorry, Mac."

Mac rubbed my back, pulling me up into his lap as I cried. "Shhh. I know. I understand." He kissed my hair again. "It's all right."

I don't know how long he held me like that, but his arms round me never loosened, never let go, not for a moment. And eventually, I was done crying.

"What happens now?" I asked, rubbing my eyes. There was still so much to think about. Maybe Mac didn't hate me as much as I'd thought he would, but that didn't change the fact that everyone knew. I still had to face teachers and social workers and what to do about Mum and...

Mac smiled and kissed my forehead. "You get a good night's sleep. You've got an apprenticeship to win tomorrow."

I took a deep breath. Maybe I just needed to take things one step at a time. I couldn't do anything right now about the decisions that would be made about my life, if my secrets got back to the school. But I could fight for the apprenticeship. The way the last couple of weeks had gone, I knew I'd need to be on top form to beat the others. They all wanted it, just as much as we did. But I didn't say that. "You too," I said instead. "You have to fight for it as well."

"I will," he promised. "If they let me." Then he was away at the window, climbing back out on to the garage roof. "I'll see you tomorrow."

I nodded. He would. Because I wasn't giving up this apprenticeship – or my friends – without a fight.

CINNAMON ROLLS

1. Heat the oven to 180°C/fan 160°C/gas 4.

2. Mix 375g of plain flour, 3 tsp of baking powder, a pinch of salt, 3 tbsp of caster sugar and 2 tsp of ground cinnamon together in a bowl.

3. Whisk 100g of melted butter together with 2 egg yolks and 200ml of milk.

4. Combine with the dry ingredients to make a soft dough, adding a little more flour if needed.

5. Turn out on to a large piece of greaseproof paper, sprinkled with flour, and press out to a rectangle shape approx. 30 x 25cm.

6. For the filling, mix together 2 tsp of ground cinnamon, 55g of soft brown sugar, 3 tbsp of caster sugar and 2 tbsp of melted butter.

7. Spread evenly over the dough and roll up the long side to make a log.

8. Cut into 8 slices and pack into a greased and lined 20-cm round tin.

9.   Brush the top with a little extra milk and bake for 30 to 35 minutes or until golden brown.
10. Remove from the oven and cool for 5 minutes, then take out of the tin.
11. For the icing, sift 125g of icing sugar into a large bowl and make a well in the centre.
12. Place 2 tbsp of cream cheese and 1 tbsp of butter in the centre, then pour over 2 tbsp of boiling water and stir to mix.
13. Add a few drops of extra boiling water until the frosting is thick enough to coat the back of a spoon.
14. Stir in 1 tsp of vanilla essence, then drizzle the icing over the rolls.

Mac met me at my door the next morning, and his hand in mine was the only thing that gave me the confidence to walk up the hill to the White Hill Bakery. Mr Carroll stood, glowering, by the door when we entered, but Miss Anderson beamed as she left Julien at the counter to welcome us.

"I'm so glad to see you both here," she said.

"I'm just glad we're allowed," Mac replied.

"Me too. And trust me, it took some pretty fast talking. This might not be an official school competition, but it's still Bake Club business, and you're still on probation, pending an official hearing. But it looks like you'll be able to sit your exams, at least." Miss Anderson shook her head. "I told the school board when I took over that we needed to replace those ovens. They were always a fire hazard. Not that I'm condoning your breaking and entering, either, mind…"

"I know, I know," Mac said. "Lesson well and

truly learned there, don't worry."

Miss Anderson turned to me. "And Lottie. How are you?"

I tried a smile. It didn't actually hurt. "OK, I guess. I think I just want to get this over with now."

"You'll be great," she said, and turned back towards Julien. "And now we're all here, I guess it's time to start."

Julien raised his eyebrows. "Ready? Then let's go and find your friends."

Jasper, Ella, Yasmin and Grace were already in the kitchen part of the bakery, aprons on and ready to bake. They all stared, of course, but really, what did I expect? Mac stuck close behind me, his hand at my waist, and I knew no one would dare say anything. Not until I was ready.

And not until the baking was done.

"Your challenge today," Julien said, as Miss Anderson handed Mac and me our aprons, "is to bake me something special. Something you think would sell well here at the White Hill Bakery. Something that makes my taste buds beg for more. You've got all day, if you need it. It's Sunday, the bakery is closed. Just remember that some staff will be in this evening to prep for tomorrow – so I suggest you finish by then."

"When will we find out who's won?" Grace asked.

Julien glanced back at Miss Anderson. "I understand that you've got an end-of-term assembly next week. That seemed an appropriate time to announce my new apprentice."

I bit back a groan. Next week? How could I wait that long?

"So, when you're ready ... get baking!"

Without the time limits of the Schools' Bake-Off, there was less of a panicked start. Instead, we all found a space to work, sorted out our recipes and ingredients and got going in our own time. I caught glimpses of what the others were doing, while I was hunting for equipment in unfamiliar cupboards, but mostly I focused on my own work.

I'd thought long and hard about what to bake for Julien. I wanted something spectacular, something unique. But I also wanted something I knew I could make, perfectly, under pressure.

In the end, I'd settled for my dad's cinnamon rolls – the breakfast he'd made for me every weekend for years. They needed to be made in stages: first the dough, then the filling, then the icing. I liked the familiar smell of the cinnamon and the fiddly rolling up and cutting. It reminded me of Dad.

Of course, by the time they were finally in the oven, everyone else was finishing up too. And apparently they'd decided it was time to talk.

I looked from face to face as they gathered round me. "Um … sorry I yelled at you all," I said.

Mac, pecan loaf still baking, came and stood beside me.

"That's OK," Ella said, overly cheerful. "We shouldn't have—"

"Yes, we should," Jasper said. "She's our friend. We did exactly what we should have done. Checked up on her. If she hadn't been lying to us for the last six months, it wouldn't have been a problem."

I winced. I had making up to do with Jasper. "Yeah. Sorry about that too."

"How's it going in here?" Miss Anderson asked, and we all turned to look at her.

I glanced up at my timer. "Another ten minutes for mine."

"Twenty for me," Mac added.

"Then you'd better get clearing up, hadn't you?" Miss Anderson said. "And when you're done, Mr Carroll has brought the school minibus round to take you all home."

My cinnamon rolls came out of the oven glossy and golden brown, and I piped bright white icing on to them, before laying them out for Julien to taste. Wiping down the counter, I knew I'd done all I could. Now I just had to wait.

And while I was waiting, there was something else I needed to take care of.

I found Jasper out in the front of the bakery, sitting at one of the little tables in the window, staring out at the street.

Sliding into the chair opposite, I said, "I really am sorry." He didn't look at me, so I went on, "I've been a rubbish friend, I know that. There's been so much going on this term and I should have been there for you, I should have … I don't know. Helped more, I guess. With Ella. Or your parents." I was guessing, now. But I wanted to do whatever I could to make Jasper forgive me. I realized now that over the past few months he had become my best friend and he deserved more.

"You should have told me the truth," he said, turning away from the window to look at me at last. "I get that you were scared, Lottie, and I get that you thought you couldn't tell anyone. But I knew you were lying about something. I knew that something was wrong, and I wanted to help. Do you know how bad it feels when your friend is hurting and you can't do anything to make it better?" I shook my head, and Jasper sighed. "Well, you're going to find out. Ella's leaving, as soon as school finishes for the holidays."

"Oh, Jasper. I'm sorry." I reached out and took his hand.

"Yeah, well. So I'm going to need you to be a much better friend."

I nodded so fast I felt a little dizzy, I was so relieved. "I will. I promise. I'll make it up to you."

Jasper gave me a half-smile and squeezed my fingers before letting go. "OK, then. Lets stop all the mushy stuff before that boyfriend of yours gets the wrong idea."

Looking up, I saw Mac standing in the doorway to the kitchens. He was smiling at us, though, so I didn't think Jasper really had anything to worry about.

"All done," he said, heading over to our table and resting his hands on my shoulders.

"Let's get going," Mr Carroll called from the door.

"What about next year?" Yasmin asked when we were all on the bus, heading back in the direction of the school and our homes. "I mean, I know we'll bake when we can next term, but we'll have our GCSEs and things, so I guess it'll be less. But what about in September? Will we carry on Bake Club?"

From the front of the coach, I heard Mr Carroll groan.

"Of course!" said Miss Anderson. "Any of you who come back for A levels will always be welcome in food tech. Well, once we have a new classroom…"

"I won't be here," Mac said.

I reached across to hold his hand and he stroked my fingers. I didn't like to think about St Mary's without Mac. But even if he got through the arson thing without expulsion, he wouldn't be coming back for A levels. That just wasn't him.

"Neither will I," added Ella, and we all turned to look at her. "Dad didn't get the office-based job. He's got to go overseas again in two weeks. I'm…" she swallowed, and Jasper wrapped an arm round her shoulders. "I'm moving in with Mum over the Easter holidays. She's got me enrolled in a local school to finish my GCSEs next year."

We were all silent at the news. It wasn't exactly a surprise for any of us, but still … Bake Club without Mac and Ella just wouldn't really be Bake Club, would it?

"We'll miss you," Yasmin said at last, and we all nodded.

I was so busy thinking about how things were going to change that it wasn't until the bus stopped that I realized Mr Carroll had parked us on Walnut Crescent. Just outside my house.

"Everybody out," he said. "We've got work to do."

The others started to pile out, but I stopped, right in the middle of the aisle. "I don't understand, sir," I said, the fear and shame rising up again. "What are we doing here? We don't need—"

"Mrs Tyler called me," he said, cutting me off. "She thought we might all be able to help you out a bit." He shook his head. "I'm sorry, Lottie. I let you down. I should have seen … should have done more. But I've been trying to tell you for six months, you don't have to do everything on your own."

I bit my lip and looked out of the window. On my front lawn stood Mrs Tyler, bin bag in hand, pointing at piles of Stuff she'd laid out on the grass. And she wasn't alone. Jasper's mum was there too, that calming face I'd seen at the police station in evidence again. She might be an expert on teens, but apparently she was up for helping adults as well.

Mum was fluttering around, looking uncertain, and as I stepped out on to the pavement, I heard her constant stream of justification. "But what if I need it one day? And we can't get rid of that – it's an heirloom. Not mine, but somebody's. It would be wrong to throw it away."

My stomach tightened. Mum must hate this. But then I heard Jasper's mum talking soothingly to her. "We'll keep the most important things, of course," she said. "And like I promised you at the start, we won't get rid of anything you're not ready to part with. But remember our questions. Do you think that someone else might need that more than you? Or that you might need the space more than you need the object? What's it really worth?"

Mum shook her head again, but Mrs Tyler already had two full bin bags behind her, so Mum must have agreed to getting rid of some Stuff, at least.

There was still a long way to go. But as Jasper and Ella, and Grace and Yasmin all picked up bin bags and started getting rid of the actual rubbish – the takeaway cartons, the broken things, the tins – I could start to see my house underneath it all again. My life, not buried in Stuff.

"Can I take some of these for my sister-in-law?" Yasmin asked, holding up a stack of cooking magazines. "She loves cooking."

Mum dashed over towards her, probably about to embark on a story of their provenance. But maybe she'd let Yasmin take one. Perhaps even two.

Maybe this was the start of something, of a change, at last.

"Come on," Mac said, tugging on my hand. "We'll make a start in the kitchen."

Glancing back at Mr Carroll, I said, "Thank you."

He shrugged. "It's what I'm here for."

The last day of term before the Easter holidays, before Year Eleven started exam prep, study leave and GCSEs, was always the day of the prize-giving assembly at St Mary's. All the Year Elevens gathered in the hall to celebrate the achievements of the last five years at school, and especially the last two terms. Parents were invited, siblings from younger classes, the whole thing. It was a pretty big event.

And this year, against the odds, Bake Club were being honoured for our achievements in the Schools' Bake-Off competition and our catering at school events.

Including, it turned out, the prize-giving assembly.

The food tech classroom was still being repaired but we were allowed to use the canteen kitchen that morning instead. We all gathered there early and soon we were turning out cinnamon rolls, croissants and muffins that the White Hill Bakery would be proud of.

Nerves were jangling and tensions rising as we carried our trays through to the hall. It was already filling up and we each went to sit with our own families. Ella was there, despite not actually being a Year Eleven, sitting with her dad. Since she was a Bake Club member and it was her last assembly, Mr Carroll had agreed she deserved to attend. Jasper slipped into a seat between his mum and dad, and Grace did the same with her parents. Yasmin's family took up the entire middle row, and Yasmin beamed and chattered with all of them.

Mac's dad and brother were nowhere to be seen, but when I asked about them, he just shook his head. "Working, I guess."

"Come and sit with us, then," I said, motioning towards where my mum sat, in the back row.

Yeah, my mum. Out of the house. Looking like a normal human being, not an amalgamation of charity shops. She was still a long way from normal – as our still ridiculously cluttered house attested – but she was trying. And that was all I'd ever really wanted.

One by one, students were called up on to the stage, their accomplishments recognized. Poetry competitions, concerts, science prizes. Then, finally, it was our turn.

We traipsed up in single file as Mr Carroll called on Miss Anderson to tell everyone about the group and what we'd achieved. Some of the things she mentioned I hadn't even realized she knew about – the mince pies for Ella's gran's church, for one. But the audience listened, applauded and looked impressed. Like we'd done something worthwhile, even if mostly what we'd done was eat a lot of cake.

"And finally," Miss Anderson said, grinning, "I'd like to welcome to the stage Julien, from the White Hill Bakery, to announce the winner of a prestigious apprenticeship at his bakery this summer."

We all clapped Julien as he came up on to the stage, but the moment we finished, Mac grabbed my hand. Right there, in front of the whole year group. I knew then, whatever he said, he still wanted this apprenticeship, and he was scared.

So was I.

I held my breath as Julien began to speak. "I've had the pleasure this year to bake with all of these students, to taste their creations, offer them tips and advice, and watch them become great bakers. Any one of them would be an asset to the White Hill Bakery. But there's only one apprenticeship. And the winner of that is…" I squeezed Mac's hand. "Lottie Hansen."

My heart fell into my stomach the moment I heard my name. Then Jasper and Yaamin were hugging me, and it was just like the Schools' Bake-Off all over again except this time, I couldn't win with Mac.

It only took moments to get us all off the stage and then it was over. Parents started tucking into the pastries and people kept trying to talk to me, but all I wanted was to talk to Mac. To say I was sorry and that we'd figure it out somehow. But where the hell was he?

"I think you'll find Mr Macintyre outside," Mr Carroll said from beside me. When I glanced up he was frowning, but he looked more resigned to the idea than annoyed.

"Thanks," I called, as I dashed out of the side door.

Mr Carroll was right, Mac was outside. But he wasn't alone. He was with Julien and Miss Anderson.

Perfect. I could kill two birds with one stone.

"Julien," I said, as I approached. "I really do appreciate this opportunity, but I think that Mac would be a better fit."

Mac rolled his eyes at me.

"Hey." I playfully punched him in the arm. "I'm trying to do a nice thing here."

Julien chuckled. "While I understand your point, Lottie, I'm afraid Mac won't be suitable for the apprenticeship."

"Why not? He's a great baker. He's much better at bread and savouries than me. And early mornings for that matter."

"All true," Mac said. "But I can't do it. I already have a job."

"At the garage?" After everything we'd been through, and we were right back where we started. "Really? You can't!"

Julien burst out laughing. "You know, this really doesn't bode well for the summer ahead."

"What do you mean?" I asked, frustration leaking out in my voice.

"I can't take the apprenticeship," Mac said slowly, as if talking to a child, "because I already have a job at the White Hill Bakery. Julien just hired me. I'll work full-time over the summer, then part-time from September, while I study at the catering college. There's a flat above the bakery too, if I need it, once I break the news to Dad..."

"Really?" It seemed too good to be true.

"Really," Julien confirmed. "I couldn't pick between you. Like you say, you both have different strengths and your very lovely teacher suggested this might be a possible solution."

"Thank you," I said.

Julien smiled. "You earned it. And you'll both be working very hard. Especially while we're all in Paris..."

I turned to Mac. "We're going to be working

together. Baking together."

"All summer," he confirmed, with a grin.

"All summer," I echoed. And then I was up on tiptoes and we were kissing again. In front of the whole school – parents, teachers, Julien, my mother, – everyone. And I didn't care who was watching, or that we had exams in a few weeks, or that Mum was still clinging on to piles of Stuff at home.

For that moment, none of it mattered. Because I had a whole sparkling, sugar-sweet summer ahead, baking with Will Macintyre.

ACKNOWLEDGEMENTS

I had a lot of help while working on this book, and I'd like to thank everyone who listened to me chatter on and on about Mac and Lottie while I was working on it! But particular thanks is due to:

My mum, for providing so many of the recipes, and making the chocolate birthday cake with magical frosting for every family birthday for years.

Grandma Whitley, for her wonderful recipe notebooks that gave me, among other things, my gingerbread recipe.

Grandma Cannon, for countless Saturday afternoon teas with wonderful cakes and sweets, inspiring a lifelong love of home-baked treats.

My husband, Simon, for rescuing the Easter roast when I was deep in revisions, for the mug, and much, much more.

My daughter, Holly, for all the lemon pie research she undertook with me.

My dad, for our many experiments with pies and pastry.

My brothers, Kip and Mike, for their unexpected enthusiasm for baking, and their chocolate ganache and lemon drizzle cakes respectively.

My cousin Sancha, a real life Miss Anderson, for

all her advice and input.

My editor, Ruth, for believing in this book and helping me make it better.

Everyone at Stripes for baking (and eating) all the recipes in the book. I appreciate the sacrifice, guys.

All my family and friends, for their constant support and belief.

The first readers, especially Team Cooper, for their enthusiasm and excitement.

And last, but not least, my agent Gemma, for everything from helping me brainstorm the book over coffee and cake, suffering through my first drafts, and texting me photos of mixing bowls that made her think of Mac, to getting the book where it is today – in your hands.

I couldn't have done it without every one of you. Thank you all.

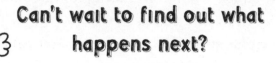

Are you a *Lottie* and MAC fan?

Can't wait to find out what happens next?

Check out Katy Cannon's website for all the inside gossip and news about Lottie, Mac and the rest of Bake Club.

- More great recipes to download – for FREE

- Get behind-the-scenes info direct from the author

- Sign up to be one of the first to receive details of the next book: *Secrets, Schemes & Sewing Machines*

- Competitions, author interviews, events and more…

www.katycannon.com

Join the conversation #lottie4mac

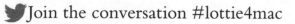

Win a D.I.Y. Cooking Party for you and five friends!

If you love to bake or are eager to start, we have a **D.I.Y. Cooking Party in a Box** to give away, courtesy of the **Beverley Glock Cookery School!** The kit has everything you need to host a brilliant baking party. You will also win a signed copy of *Love, Lies & Lemon Pies* for you and each of your friends.

The kit includes:

"How to run a cooking party and stay sane" guide

Party invitations

Recipe cards including sweet scones,
homemade lemonade and Beverley's
Surprise chocolate cupcakes

Ingredients and utensils list, so you
can get everything you need

Cotton aprons and fabric pens
to customize your apron

Chef hats

Cake cases

Cake decorations

Cake stand

Napkins and paper plates

Truly Scrumptious Teapot Vase

Party bags

Ten runners up will win Beverley's app and a signed copy of *Love, Lies & Lemon Pies*!

The iPad app, **Cupcakes, Muffins and Afternoon Tea**, provides over sixty imaginative recipes, plus professional tips and a video tutorial. You can also use it to store baking notes and favourite recipes, and to share your creations with your friends!

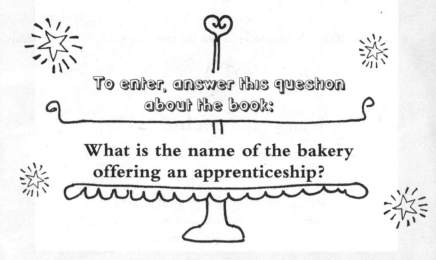

To enter, answer this question about the book:

What is the name of the bakery offering an apprenticeship?

Send us your answer via email to **publicity@littletiger.co.uk** with your name and age. The competition ends 31st August 2014. Terms and conditions can be found on our website:
www.littletiger.co.uk

BEVERLEY GLOCK Cookery School
www.beverleyglock.com
www.facebook.com/beverleyglockcookeryschool
www.youtube.com/beverleyglock
Twitter: @beverleyglock

BEVERLEY
GLOCK

Secrets, Schemes & Sewing Machines

Out February 2015

Grace: This was supposed to be Grace's starring year, until she opened the door to a family secret that changed everything. Now she's stuck making costumes in Sewing Club and watching someone else play the lead role – unless she can find a way to win it back.

CONNOR: Far from home and exiled to a new school, all Connor wants is to keep a low profile and get through the year. But agreeing to help his step-dad out with the school play means he's soon caught up in Grace's schemes.

Grace had a plan for this year – and it didn't involve learning to sew. But being out of the spotlight isn't the disaster she imagined, even if Connor is convinced she's still a diva extraordinaire. Can Grace prove she's really changed and save the play from the sidelines, even though her family is coming apart at the seams?

ABOUT THE AUTHOR

Katy Cannon was born in the United Arab Emirates, grew up in North Wales and now lives in Hertfordshire, which is rather flat and green by comparison. When she was eleven, she had appendicitis and spent the two-week recovery period reading constantly. After that, she never really stopped.

Katy loves to bake, but isn't very good at following recipes. Her cakes and bakes always seem to need just an extra pinch of this, or a little more of that – and they always taste better for it! Her husband and five-year-old daughter are her very willing taste testers. They particularly recommend Mac's chocolate brownies.

www.katycannon.com